To all the soldiers out there who stand between dangers to protect their nation.

Chapter I

"If you feel pain, you're alive. If you feel other people's pain, you're a human being" –Leo Tolstoy

The steam from the boiling pasta brushed against my face, moist and suffocating. It hadn't been long since the news broke of warfare in Herdonia, yet no one knew if it would continue. My stepmother lounged on the couch, pleased as images of bombed hospitals, dead bodies, and kidnapped children flashed across the screen. *Till we meet again,* the TV said.

You might be wondering what awful human being would feel satisfied at this view. But that is where I correct you, my stepmother isn't a human being, but a monster in my eyes.

I reached for a spoon and gently stirred the pot to check if the pasta was ready. After turning off the stove, I poured the noodles into the strainer.

"Ouch," I muttered, as the boiling water stung my skin. "Food's ready, like you asked," I said flatly. Stepmother shot me a look of disgust. I closed my eyes, wishing she'd vanish—but of course, she remained.

"Well, that took you long enough. Ford and Dixie waited a long time." Her eyebrows furrowed, and she stormed off. I stared as the steam curled toward the ceiling, then began plating the food.

"Mom!" Ford howled. "Dixie said she's getting the new clothes I asked for!" Ford glanced at me with sorrowful eyes.

"Mama, he's lying!" Dixie screeched, nearly causing me to drop a plate.

Without a word, stepmother slipped a white piece of paper into a cabinet. "Nonsense, children. You'll both get new wardrobes. To the table now," she said.

"Should I add more salt?" I asked quietly as I took my seat.

"Don't you think you've caused enough trouble, young lady?" Her eyes flared with sharp judgment.

"I suppose so."

For years, I've been trying to find the words to speak up for liberty. I remember when I was little—it wasn't a daily ritual to be yelled at. Stepmother used to love me once. That love never really left my soul.

Since the age of seven, I've been shuffled through foster homes after an orphanage found me wandering the streets. I never minded walking with an empty stomach or sleeping on cold sidewalks. I found it oddly blissful.

I'll never forget the boy who brought me an apple every morning. He had golden-blond hair and the most mesmerizing blue eyes. At nine, I was finally adopted.

But something changed. She grew crueler. It all started after I turned ten, when everything spiraled. I even remember practicing arguments in the mirror.

I left the table and descended to the basement, where my cold, shallow room welcomed me. I sat on Ford's old bed—not very comfortable. The only thing I had from my parents was a worn Polaroid of Herdonia in summer. It wasn't much, but it meant everything to me.

The front door creaked open. With each thudding step, dust trickled from the ceiling into my hair. It was my stepfather. His wages weren't much, yet he somehow managed lavish gifts for Ford and Dixie.

I went upstairs for a glass of water—I had nothing to eat.

"Ain't that crazy, Bill? I mean, they could always take the little brat if they wanted to, but not *my* kids," stepmother said. My small footsteps couldn't escape my stepfather's sharp ears.

"Why are you up here? You should be downstairs, sleeping," he snapped.

"It's only seven-thirty, sir." I glanced up at his blazing, dark eyes.

"Go back downstairs!" I lowered my gaze and gripped the cold doorknob.

Staring out the small basement window, I could only see the dark sky and creeping grass overtaking foggy clouds. I looked at the rusted clock above my bed. 12:45.
Suddenly, a shadow appeared behind the glass. Not surprising—it was Peter, my childhood best friend and the gardener's son. He always found a way to sneak in. We met on his father's first day of work. I was watching Ford and Dixie play outside through the window when Peter wandered in, looking for the bathroom. We just clicked.

I opened the window. His handsome face peeked in as he climbed through.

"As much as I hate how you sneak in, I'll never tire of it," I told him.

"It drives me nuts that I live just a few blocks away and still have to pull this crap, Alice."

"I know it annoys you." Smiling, he dug into his pocket and handed me something—a bracelet.

"What's this for?"

"I bought it with the dollar I found on the street."

I hugged him and slipped the bracelet on. Peter was nineteen, two years older than me. We shared the same hatred for my parents, and one day, he promised we'd run away and start fresh somewhere far away.

"I have to go. My mom's sick, and I promised I'd bring her medicine. Goodbye, Alice."

"Goodbye, Peter." I waved.

Almost six hours passed. Everyone should have been asleep. My stomach screamed for food—I hadn't eaten a full meal in five days. I dragged my weak legs up the basement steps. The door wasn't loud by day, but at night, it moaned louder than my stepfather's snoring. I opened it cautiously and looked around. Nobody.

The kitchen was littered with leftovers. The pasta I had labored over on an empty stomach was now smeared across four plates. I couldn't turn on the lights—I'd be beaten if caught.

A hole in the pocket of my sweatpants was wide enough to let me dig out the Polaroid. My eyes searched the remains of dinner. I grabbed a used fork. I didn't care if it was filthy. *I didn't care.* The fork scraped pasta onto my tongue. I licked the plate until my face stared back at me. My cheeks bore belt marks. I'd need to use my last ten dollars on foundation just to hide them.

I remembered each lash. Then my mind flashed to the white paper stepmother placed in the living room cabinet. Without thinking, my legs moved toward it.

Have you ever let curiosity get the best of you?

I just did.

Chapter II

"There's a rebel lying deep in my soul"-Clint Eastwood

I opened the envelope and read the letter:

ORDER TO REPORT FOR INDUCTION

Date: July 21, 1992
From: Herdonia's Official Forces
Brigadier General Philip Haven
Room Number: 1187
To: Rogers Family

This is a potential military draft. We request your child to assume a position in Herdonia's Official Forces. Due to growing demands and shortfall in recruitment, only a few positions remain.
Eligibility requires reaching the age of majority. Flight accommodations are included with two tickets. An attached form on the back page outlines group base assignments.

Confirmation of service implies:

1. He/she will be at risk.
2. He/she may be disqualified if criteria are unmet.
3. He/she will be stationed based on individual skill sets.
4. He/she must pledge loyalty.

Upon agreement, travel via Whisperwind Station to access military flights.

May G-d be with you.
Best of luck,
Philip Haven

I stared at the letter in disbelief, sweat gathering in my trembling hand. Slowly, I shut the cabinet and crept back to my room. The silence was deafening. I lay on my bed, eyes locked on the old clock ticking above.

Did she want me to leave? Was this her way of saying "go"—of handing me off to war like an unwanted package? My heart thudded as I read the letter again. *At risk.* That phrase echoed in my mind.

I rose and searched for a bag. Anything that could carry what little I owned. I found my toothbrush and the crusted toothpaste I hadn't replaced in months. Clothes—nothing but worn hand-me-downs from Ford and Dixie—were shoved deep into the bag to make room for other essentials. I didn't want to be part of a war, but it felt safer than staying here.

I folded my sweatshirt—the only thing I bought with my own money after three years of saving—and tucked it in gently. The train station's name glinted from the bottom of the page: *Whisperwind Station.*

Moving silently, I tiptoed up the basement stairs, avoiding any creak that could betray me. I halted at the front door, remembering the house alarm. A chill ran down my spine. I turned toward the kitchen, held my breath, and disabled the alarm.

I grabbed a notepad and pen. My fingers hesitated, but I scribbled a note. No tears. No second thoughts.

I opened the door and walked out into the night.

Chapter III

"The heart of a mother is a deep abyss at the bottom of which you will find forgiveness"-Honore de Balzac

The train station was a twenty-five minute walk from my house. The streets were empty, but far-off car engines hummed through the silence. I ran to Peter's place. All the lights were off. I slid my letter into his mailbox and wrote in bold: *FOR PETER ONLY.*

By the time I arrived at the station, people were already boarding. I spotted kids laughing, lugging heavy suitcases and oversized bags. They looked ready for summer camp—not war.

"Mom, I don't want to go!" sobbed a boy about my age. I'm seventeen now. His eyes were wide with panic, and his voice trembled like it didn't belong to him. His mother replied softly in Herodian, trying to soothe him. I passed them and stepped onto the train. The boy followed, still crying, then collapsed into his seat, silent. He didn't look like someone fit to be drafted. Something felt off. The train was crowded. Teenagers clutched their draft letters, comparing group assignments and chatting nervously.

"I'm Joseph," said a boy next to me, way too cheerful for 4:30 A.M. "You are?"

"I'm Alice," I mumbled, my exhaustion flattening my voice. I avoided eye contact. His blond waves brushed his forehead, freckles dotted his tan skin, and his enormous blue eyes watched me with fascination. He was tall—maybe even beautiful

"Do you think you'll be accepted?" he asked eagerly.

"Accepted for what?"

"They're only taking three soldiers."

My heart started racing. That number echoed like a threat. *Three.* My mind reeled through consequences—being rejected, sent back home, screamed at for sneaking out, punished for breathing wrong. I clutched my ragged bag stuffed with hand-me-downs, stale supplies, and a broken watch.

Joseph reached into his brown duffel and pulled out a half-eaten granola bar.

"Where are you from, Alice?"

I stared at him, crumbs sprinkling his seat. I knew little about my birth parents—only scraps from my adoption certificate.

"My parents are originally from Herdonia," I said. "They moved here when I was born."

I didn't add anything more. My brain warned me: *Stay quiet.*

We sat in silence for twenty minutes. He kept drumming his fingers on his luggage—a slow, annoying rhythm.

"Can you please stop?" I snapped.

He raised his eyebrows and let out a soft laugh.

"What?"

"Why do you get annoyed so quickly?"

The teasing curled at the corner of his mouth. He was enjoying this. It was obvious.

Suddenly, the train screeched to a stop. I grabbed the nearest pole to steady myself, but Joseph crashed face-first along with his bag.

"My nose!" he groaned, sitting cross-legged on the floor, hands covering his face, rocking back and forth.

"Move your hand."

He hesitated, then slowly peeled it away. No blood. Just a bright red flush.

"You're fine, you wuss. There's no blood."

I stood up to exit the train, my arms and legs aching from the ride. My whole body felt hollow with fatigue. Even my eyes betrayed me—drooping under the weight of everything I was carrying

Chapter IV

"Deep in every heart slumbers a dream, and the couturier knows it: every woman is a princess"-Christian Dior

The airport was immense. I'd only flown once before—when my parents left me. The memory made my throat tighten.

Inside, warmth wrapped around me, a stark contrast to the cold outside. A man in a navy blue suit stood near the entrance. His gold name tag read *John,* and his ridiculous purple bowtie matched his obnoxious smile.

"Um... can you help me with boarding?" I asked. He looked at me with a weird, too-innocent expression. I didn't trust it.

"First time? Flying alone, young lady?" That phrase— *young lady*—scraped through my head like fingernails across my childhood. Stepmother used to spit it like venom.

"I'm flying to Herdonia. With Herdonia's Official Forces." I followed his pointed finger to a line of teens dressed in military suits. Joseph stood near the end.

"Oh, thanks," I muttered, dragging my feet toward the group.

"Did you get lost?" Joseph called out, smirking.

"I didn't get lost, Joseph. I went to the restroom," I snapped. Lie. I hated his teasing—so aggravating.

I caught sight of an old woman scowling in our direction, her expression twisted like she'd just swallowed spoiled milk. Bleached hair, deep-set wrinkles, and a mouth set like stone. I looked away.

"Flight to Elarion 302, please have your boarding passes ready." A sudden rush of bodies surged toward the gate. *What's in Elarion? A better reality?*

Then came him—a broad-shouldered man with thick eyebrows that shadowed his glaring eyes. He didn't look like someone who tolerated nonsense.

"Our flight is leaving soon. Gather your supplies," he barked. He stopped in front of the boy I'd noticed earlier—the one who cried at the station.

"How old are you?" he asked. The boy didn't respond—just fiddled with his fingers, eyes glued to the floor.

"Is he abnormal?" the man asked, bluntly.

"He's autistic," Joseph cut in, defensive. "He's my brother. Give him a chance."

The man studied Joseph for a moment, then stepped into the center of the group.

"My name is Chief Flow. I will be your commander." His voice carried weight, dragging attention like iron.

I stood silently as travelers drifted past, giving us looks I recognized too well. Judging. Wondering. *Where are these kids headed—off to die?* I wasn't heading to war. I was escaping a battlefield I was born into.

"Flight HA 403, boarding now."

I gripped my bag and followed Chief Flow. The boarding tunnel felt eerie—long, narrow, like the hallways in those haunted hotels I hated. The kind that made you feel watched.

"I've always wanted to go to Herdonia," Joseph said behind me. "So hot there. So cold here in Nuvoria. This flight's gonna take a while—"

"That's nice, but I'm tired," I interrupted. "Please keep it down."

He rolled his eyes and looked back. "Connor, come sit next to me," he called out. The boy—his little brother—tugged at his sleeve, walking close.

"He's my little brother," Joseph said. "My older one's in college, couldn't come." Joseph packed away his luggage roughly, his protective arm briefly around Connor.

"Are you scared for your brother?" I asked.

"I don't know," he replied.

"He thinks differently."

"And? So what? You don't have any power over that," he snapped.

I didn't answer. I didn't want a fight—not now. The exhaustion pressed against my chest. No sleep. Twelve hours of sitting next to Joseph and Connor. And too many unfamiliar faces staring back like ghosts waiting to form stories.

Chapter V

"To knock a thing down, especially if it is cocked at an arrogant angle, is a deep delight of the blood"-George Santayana

Connor was kind enough to let me take the window seat—though Joseph definitely forced him.

The first hour was nothing but tension. My stomach twisted after takeoff, and the vibrations rattled through my spine. I didn't hold anyone's hand. I just sat there, bracing myself. A boy behind me kept kicking my seat, jerking me forward each time.

I closed my eyes. But I wasn't dreaming.

I remembered being eleven. The only memory I have from that age. Dixie and Ford had just received new bicycles— shiny, bright, and perfect. I was trying to help clean up the trash, towering over me like a monster. Somehow, I managed to shove it into the bin.

"Can I ride?" I'd asked stepmother. A mistake.

"No! Never. They're supposed to have fun. You stay behind their shadows, do you hear me, Alice?" I cried. She didn't care. Just grabbed me by the shirt and dragged me to my room.

The plane finally landed after brutal turbulence—the wind slicing through our descent. The extra hour it took to reach Herdonia only made me sicker.

My legs trembled as I climbed out of my seat, backpack dragging on my shoulder. The airport was heavy with heat, and my sweatshirt—old and worn—clung to my soaked skin. I fidgeted with the torn hole near its pocket.

"All right, the bus will be here shortly. It's a thirty-minute ride to base, where you'll be assigned bunks. Am I clear?"

Everyone answered in robotic unison: "Sir, yes, sir!"

I wondered if stepmother noticed I was gone yet.

"Joseph, I don't want to die. I want Mama," Connor whispered, trembling.

Joseph glanced around, nervous at the eyes falling on them. Then he forced a smile.

"We'll see Mama soon. I promise."

Liar, I thought. That boy made too many promises. Did he even believe them himself?

Two boys rushed past me. I recognized one—he'd kicked my seat for the entire flight. Maybe next time I'll return the favor.

The bus ride was silent. *Deathening,* like everything held its breath. When we arrived, the sun slapped me across the face. The air felt thicker than before. We were in the middle of a desert—military bases rising like ghosts from the sand.

"Bunk Number One: Group A. If you're unsure of your group, check the back of your letter."

I dug through my backpack, searching for the crumpled paper. Buried deep, I finally found it. *Group C.*

Everyone else was already heading toward their bunks. I was alone.

I ran to catch up, but the sand scorched my feet through my torn shoes.

"That burns!" I hissed, wobbling toward the bunks in tiny, reluctant steps.

"Uh—sir?" Chief Flow towered over me.

He shot me a glare, snatched my letter, and pointed toward my bunk.

Inside stood a girl with golden blond hair pulled into a severe bun, thick pants hugging her legs, and a black tank top that made her look like she belonged here.

I approached slowly.

"You're new?" she asked.

I gave her a half-smile and nodded, avoiding her eyes. Her accent was strong—too cheery. I didn't like it.

"Do you know where I can get the uniform?"

She opened the door and pointed to the top bunk. Neatly folded army clothes lay across the bed.

"Thanks." I walked past her, head down on purpose. No eye contact. The bunk smelled dry—like my room back home. Cold. Stale.

Top bunk. A small victory.

There were a few girls in the room, all staring at me. Maybe it was the sweat—the way it poured off me like rain that didn't belong in this desert.

They definitely have been in the army longer than they could remember.

Chapter VI

"Don't ever promise more than you can deliver, but always deliver more than you can promise"-Lou Holtz

"Is somebody in the restroom? I need to change." The girls only shook their heads. No words.

I gathered my supplies and stepped inside. The black tank top clung tightly to me, uncomfortable against my skin. The green pants were oversized, heavy with clunky pockets. I hated them. A badge with the flag of Herdonia was stitched near my chest. I stepped into thick black boots—too big, but I didn't have the guts to ask for smaller ones. They felt like they were made for trekking through mud. Was that the point?

Outside the restroom, I felt slightly cleaner. I reached for my old watch, brushing sand off the face— The door slammed open.

"Shooting drills!" Chief barked.

Everyone scattered, stepping lightly toward the metal field door. His eyes locked on my watch.

"Put the watch away," he said, low but firm.

"Can I just check the time? It'll only take a sec—"

"Not listening, are we?" He snatched the watch. Threw it across the room. Plastic and glass burst into the air.

"What was that for?" He stared me down with eyes that didn't blink.

Note Number One: Never yell at your military chief. He will eat you alive.

"Out of this bunk. Now, Ms. Rogers!"

I rose slowly, blinking back heat and fury. The watch lay shattered in the corner. I stepped out into the scorching sun—no shade, no mercy.

I fell into line beside the other soldiers. My hat dug into my bun like punishment. Sweat pooled beneath my shirt. "Do you think we're actually shooting guns?" Joseph asked, his shirt soaked through.

Chief returned, flanked by generals. A large cart rolled up, loaded with weapons.

Heavy rifles were handed out. I barely knew what to do with mine—it was the first time I'd ever held one. I'd spent most of my life inside, forgotten.

Joseph and Connor laughed, aiming playfully at distant targets. "First," Chief instructed, "hold the gun against your chest with both hands on the upper bar."

I flinched. It was too close to my face. Connor fumbled and toppled to the ground, the rifle landing awkwardly across him.

After more instructions, Chief walked off, handing Connor a folded map instead of a weapon. The heat was unbearable—easily over a hundred degrees.

"Alice? Is that your name?" Connor was beside me, map in hand, eyes the color of ocean glass. I nodded slowly.

"My name's Connor." His smile rounded his cheeks like a toddler's.

I tilted my head, attempting innocence. But my usual coldness probably betrayed me.

I'd never met someone autistic before.

"Why does he have a map?" I whispered to Joseph.

"Chief wants him to memorize Valkros. His memory's insane. Everyone says he'll go far—photographic brain and all." Valkros: the place we were headed to fight for peace.

I turned back to my weapon.

CRACK!

The sound made me jump, but my shot hit the mark. Joseph aimed next—

CRACK!

 Straight into the sand.

Others started aiming at each other, joking like this was summer camp. When Chief returned to the field, his expression made me groan. Stepfather-level grumpy. He stormed past me, scolding one boy and snatching his gun. The boy was sent away.

"Back to bunks! It's late. I want you washed, your bunks neat, and when I enter—salute. Do you hear me?"

His glare lingered on me as he left.

"Was that for everyone or just you?" Joseph smirked. I stared at my boots. He didn't deserve a response.

"He broke my watch. I just wanted to check the time." My fists clenched. I fought the urge to swing.

Back at the bunk, the room was empty. And boiling. No A/C. No mercy.

I searched the floor. The shattered watch still glistened in the corner.

"I just wanted to check the time!" I threw my army hat on the bed, slammed my weapon down, and headed to the showers.

The water was ice cold—but blessed relief. I scrubbed every inch of skin and finished the last of my toothpaste.

I caught my reflection afterward—cheeks flushed, hair ends washed into honey strands.

Chapter VII

Mrs. Rogers

"My passion and fire run deep through my veins, my blood, there's no doubt about that"-Carolyn Aronson

"WHERE IS SHE?!" Mrs. Rogers whipped around to face Bill, slouched on the couch with a beer in one hand and the remote in the other.

"Maybe she actually went off to that army thing... like that letter said, Daniela." He lazily gestured toward the cabinet. She flung it open. Empty. Just a book and a pile of old CDs.

"Bill—Bill, she *left for the army!*" She bolted down the basement stairs, heart pounding. The bed was half-made. Dust covered everything.

"She's gone, Bill! The brat's *gone!*"

Ford meandered down the stairs and plopped beside his dad.

"What happened, Mama? Did Alice really go through with that stupid idea?"

Mrs. Rogers stormed back into the room, ignoring her son.

"Mark my words, Bill. If that girl ever comes crawling back, she's scrubbing this house top to bottom till her hands fall off!"

She stood there, seething—staring at Bill and Ford. They didn't flinch. Didn't care.

Mrs. Rogers did. More than she'd ever admit.

Alice

I got back in uniform, organized my bunk like Chief warned. I couldn't risk his fury again.

Outside, the sunset glazed the desert orange. Soldiers fired at distant targets, rifles cracking like thunder. I saw Chief marching toward my bunk. I snapped into a salute.

Like he told me. Like he asked. Like he screamed.

"Get outside. Meet up with the rest," he barked. Then his eyes dropped to my bed. My gun sat there.

Note Number Two: *Don't leave your gun unattended.*

"The most important thing in being a soldier, Ms. Rogers... IS TO NEVER LEAVE YOUR GUN UNATTENDED. DO YOU HEAR ME?"

"Sir, yes, sir!" My voice trembled under his thunderous tone, bouncing through the heat-drenched air. It rang in my ears, echoed between my ribs. He stomped off.

Anger issues.

I joined Joseph and Connor, double-checking my gun strap.

"Where've you been?" Connor's big blue eyes were oceans I wasn't ready to drown in.

I dropped my gaze to my boots. My fingers brushed against the Polaroid buried in my pocket. *Mother… Father… are you still alive?*

We entered a large room filled with rows of seats and long metal tables. Soldiers sat quietly—some whispering, others tight-lipped. I watched as Chief stood in front, posters clutched in his fists.

"Perception," he said, calm for once. "Perception is key to becoming a soldier. It's like wisdom." He scanned the room. "Raise your hand if you carry wisdom."

Connor's hand shot up, face beaming. Joseph gently placed a hand on his shoulder, grounding him.

"Thank you, Connor," Chief said with a flicker of warmth.

Then his tone shifted again—back to steel.

"I want strength."

He peeled back the posters: bloodied bodies, shell-shocked soldiers, twisted limbs frozen in terror. Gasps. A few girls clung to themselves. Even the air tightened.

"Tonight is your first night here," he said. "We'll eat. Tomorrow… I want more."

Later in the cafeteria, everything gleamed silver and sterile. Soldiers sat in perfect rows, guns snug against their backs, eating pasta and boiled vegetables like machines on break

Chapter VIII

"Start where you are. Use what you have. Do what you can"-
Arthur Ashe

I was forced to sit next to Connor and Joseph—no one
else felt safe. The cafeteria was freezing, and watching Joseph
pick up scraps of pasta with his fingertips didn't help.

"Joseph, you eat like a pig. It's disgusting."

He caught my glare, rolled his bright blue eyes.

"Oh please, Alice. We were baking out there with no
water. Let me live." Another pasta piece popped into his
mouth. Connor snorted, chewing through his carrots like they
were sacred.

"Alice, you never told us about your family. Got
siblings?"

Here we go again. I hated that question. It shattered
something soft inside me every time.

"No, I don't have siblings." Not exactly a lie. Ford and
Dixie weren't mine. Not really. Not by blood. And I had no
memory of anything different.

Joseph didn't argue. Just stared blankly—
expressionless—but I knew he saw right through me. Through
all the lies I wrapped around my ribs. I lost my appetite. The
sun earlier had drained everything I had.

"So... it's just you and Connor?"

"My mother always said, with two men in the house, she didn't need another child like Connor."

I blinked hard. What kind of mother says that?

"Connor, give it back! You already ate your carrots!"

Joseph lunged, tried to yank it out of Connor's hand. "Let me go!"

Everyone was watching. Laughing. Humiliated, I covered my face.

Connor shoved Joseph and shoved the carrot in his mouth triumphantly. "Connor, you swine!"

He stuck out his tongue—carrot bits in his teeth—and swallowed them with pride.

Ridiculous.

I grabbed a glass of water, stood up—forgetting about the monstrous gun strapped to my back.

My body jerked backward.

Gasp. Air, gone. My face went ghost-white.

And then—

CRACK. The gun fired.

A scream ripped through the cafeteria.

Generals dashed toward the sound. A girl, bleeding, was carried out. Everyone around me mumbled and stared.

"IN A LINE!"

My heart pounded so fast I saw it moving in my chest—uniform pulsing.

Up. Down. Up again.

Chief stalked down the line. No words. Just eyes.

He stopped a foot away from me. I froze.

His glare sliced through my skin.

"Come with me."

I glanced back—Joseph panicked, Connor looked ready to cry. And I walked.

We entered a building. Cold. Stark. Packed with police, a few soldiers.

"You didn't even ask if I did it!" I yelled, hands raised.

"I don't *need* to ask. I've been doing this for years. Your face said it all."

He paused. "Now tell me—how and why did you shoot that soldier?"

"I didn't *mean* to! I fell! The gun was on me—it just went off! I didn't think—I…" Tears welled up, tight and hot. *Don't cry. Don't cry. Don't cry.*

He yanked my arm and shoved me into a small, empty cell.

"You're staying here the rest of the night."

He walked away. Cold.

"What about my gun?" My voice cracked. I couldn't hold back the tears this time.

He didn't answer. Just exited through the back—my gun in hand. The only thing that might protect me.

Silence.

Cold floor beneath me—better than the lumpy beds outside. I sat in the far corner, hoping the shadows could shield me.

I remembered every time I'd complained about the heat. This cold was worse.

Then—

CRACK!

Chapter IX

"There is only one corner of the universe you can be certain of improving, and that's your own self"-Aldous Huxley

Tears of horror streamed down my cold, reddened cheeks. *Don't cry. Don't cry. Don't cry.* I stayed on my knees, frozen. Gunshots rang out. Screams. Alarms blared like sirens in my skull. I reached for my back—my gun—gone. Chief had taken it.

The cell door burst open. My brain screamed: *They're coming to kill me.* A tall figure stepped in.

It was Joseph.

"Take the gun. They're outside!"

I grabbed the weapon—cold metal against my fingers. I ran through the exit into thick, humid air... and the sick stench of blood pooled at my feet.

I dropped into a shooting stance, aimed at a shadow.

Click.

A man's leg burst red—he screamed.

CRACK. I was on the ground. My back was on fire. My veins surged. My face was crimson. My breath was gone.

I've been shot.

And the world blacked out.   A flicker. Blurred shapes. Hands. Motion. Exported somewhere. Gone again.

Memories washed over me—dizzy and vivid.

Ford and Dixie's birthday. Ford got a Star Wars LEGO set to match his themed room.

"Happy birthday, Ford," I said—still trying to be family.

He shoved me aside and ran to his father.

"Papa, I wanted the other *one. This one's stupid!" He kicked it against the wall.*

Stepfather scooped up the box and tossed it into the basement—my room. Shut the door.

Dixie held a Barbie doll—pink dress, matching bow.

"Thanks," she mumbled.

"Can I please see, Dixie?"

"No! Get away, Alice! Mama, she's trying to touch my doll!"

Their yelling tore through my ears. It was the last time I cried in front of them.

Pain. Everywhere. Dry blood on my hands. Doctors circled me. One with gray hair leaned over.

"Where am I?" I croaked.

"We need tests. We need to find the bullet and remove it." His accent wrapped around his words.

"I'm… going to have surgery?" No answer.

A needle pierced my arm.

Darkness.

Third blackout. Still hurting. Thirst choked me. *I could drink the whole ocean. I could drink the whole ocean. I could drink the whole ocean.* I repeated it like a prayer.

Footsteps. A door opened.

"You're awake!"

Light struck my eyes—I shielded them with both hands.

She stood tall, blond, with gleaming green eyes.

"What happened? Who shot me? Will I ever walk again?"

"Honey, it's very late. Food's coming soon." She paused, her voice tender. "You know… it's a miracle you woke up. Most of us thought you wouldn't make it."

"So why *am* I alive?" My voice trembled. "Why am I here? Why this pain? Why this soldier's life?"

My tears tried again. I fought them back.

"If that bullet was an inch closer to your spine, you wouldn't be talking. You wouldn't even be here."

Her voice wrapped around the room—gentle, foreign, soft. Her gold hair spilled down her back.

"Is everyone dead? Have they been shot?"

I barely whispered.

"Alice, it's late. Eat. Rest. We'll figure it out soon. I promise."

Her smile—like sunlight after a hurricane—held me together.

Chapter X

"Nobody made a greater mistake than he who did nothing because he could do only a little"-Edmund Burke

The warm sun hit my face through the window as I woke up, still confined to the hospital. I tried lifting myself with what little strength I had, but pain pulsed through my back. *Will I ever walk again? Is Joseph even alive? Where was Connor that night? Will I be sent back home?*

A nurse appeared—a blonde woman with a welcoming smile.

"If you hadn't noticed," she chimed, placing a tray of food beside me, "I'm your nurse! How do you feel, honey?"

"Will I walk again? When will I be free?" I asked.

She laughed softly. "You sure ask a lot of questions." Then after a pause, she added, "You have to be patient. But yes, I'm almost certain you'll walk again." She pulled up a chair next to my bed.

"What's your name?" I asked, staring into her eyes. Glass-green, catching sunlight like emeralds. I could see my own reflection inside them.

"Lia. My name is Lia." Her features glowed with kindness.

"Now, eat. We'll start working on your balance soon!"

Without another word, she left.

I'm starving. I'm starving. I'm starving. The food tasted rich, warming me from the inside out, pulling my thoughts away from the constant agony gnawing at my spine.

After breakfast, Lia guided me into another room. I leaned into her for support as I shuffled forward slowly. Around me, broken soldiers—wounded legs, fractured hips, immobilized necks. We all limped forward, clinging to strength and shadowed hope.

Months passed.

I waited by the hospital bed—wishing, hoping—they would come.

2:00 PM. 4:00 PM. Midnight.

Still no sign.

I couldn't sleep. The moon stared back at me, sky crystal-clear.

Are they alive? Are they alive? Are they alive? I whispered inside myself like a prayer.

I peeled off the heavy blanket, pressing against the wall to rise. The curtains revealed thousands of stars stretching out into the quiet dark.

They have to be okay. They have to be okay. I chanted silently.

Looking at my fingers, I noticed the grooves of a gun handle still etched into my skin. Swollen. Tender.

I tiptoed through the room, adjusting the brace on my back. Light from the hallway crawled through door cracks. I saw shadows moving.

The doorknob twisted.

I held still.

Slowly—quietly—the door opened.

"You up?" It was Joseph. And someone behind him.

"Joseph?" I stepped forward, my fingers grazing the bed sheets.

"I'm not supposed to be here. I snuck in. Chief wanted me to make sure you're recovering properly," he whispered, leading another person into the room.

It was Connor.

I exhaled deeply. *They're okay,* I reminded my heart.

"Why did you come so late?" I hissed, voice low.

Joseph shrugged. "Chief's orders. He's terrifying when he's mad."

Connor nodded and sat on my bed.

"Connor, off the bed—Alice needs to sit," Joseph scolded.

"It's fine," I said, standing carefully. "But… it's been a few months. Do you remember what happened that night? I blacked out."

Joseph leaned toward me, adjusting my brace gently.

"I didn't realize you'd been shot until a man collapsed. Your gun slid to my feet, and blood was pouring from your back."

My eyes widened.

"Three girls recognized you and carried you away. One got shot—I think in the arm. And after that—well—I shot the last one," he said, chest puffed.

I rolled my eyes. He was showing off again.

"Alright, hero. Then what?"

"You opened your eyes briefly. One of the girls asked me to report everything to Chief."

Connor crossed his arms, brow furrowing. "Not fair, Joseph. You got to fight!"

"Chief's orders," Joseph replied coolly. "You're not allowed to carry a gun."

Connor stood, fists clenched. "It's not fair! Not fair!"

Joseph lunged and covered Connor's mouth. But it was too late.

The door burst open.

Chapter XI

"I always prefer to believe the best of everybody, it saves so much trouble"-Rudyard Kipling

"Alice? Who are these two?" Lia's voice broke through the quiet as the lights flicked on, flooding the room with a harsh glow. I covered my eyes, blinking against it.

"I didn't mean to—" She cut me off.

"You know you're not supposed to have visitors at night." Her green eyes—sharp, calculating—swept across Joseph and Connor.

"I'm sorry, we'll leave," Joseph said quickly. "We just wanted to say hello."

"Did your commander send you?" He nodded, eyes locked on the floor, reaching instinctively for Connor's hand.

"I understand," Lia said. "But you came without permission. I'll let this slide—*just* this once. If I catch you again without clearance, there will be consequences. Got it?"

Joseph gave a tense nod, then hurried out, Connor trailing behind.

As silence settled, I watched the door close. Something about Connor's mind fascinated me—how it processed things, how it glimmered just below the surface.

"Have I met you before?" The question slipped from my lips before I could stop it. Too soft. Too raw. Lia leaned in.

"I'm sorry?"

I wanted to swallow my words whole. I shouldn't have said anything. *I should've stayed quiet. I always ruin things.*

"Never mind," I whispered. "It's nothing. I'll just go back to bed."

I eased down, staring at the linoleum floor as my mind twisted into knots.

Lia let out a long breath. I looked up.

"Well… now that you're awake, I might as well share the good news." Her voice glowed with warmth.

My heart skipped.

"Am I… good to leave?"

"Yes, honey," she said, smiling like spring sunshine, "You're being discharged first thing tomorrow morning."

Chapter XII

"You get used to sadness, growing up in the mountains, I
guess"-Loretta Lynn

I hadn't gotten much sleep. The excitement—the kind
that pulses behind your ribs—kept me up all night. Today, I'd
finally be free.

I hadn't spoken to my roommates since my first day.
And now I regret it—the bitter taste of not trying to connect,
not saying hello.

I got dressed in my uniform, the only thing I owned in
the hospital. The deep red scar along my back stung as I bent.
It felt wrong—like a wound branded into who I'd become.
Still, I reminded myself to be grateful. *I can walk.* Even if it's
with pain. Even if it's with a limp.

The door creaked open. Green eyes. Lia.

"You ready? A few people will be picking you up in
about five minutes."

"Yeah, I'm ready. Can we just go?" I dashed toward
the elevator, slapping the down button again and again. Faster.
Faster. Faster.

Lia followed with a clipboard clutched to her chest,
scribbling notes. I studied her face—dimples, and smaller than
I remembered.

"Lia, how old are you?"

She glanced up. "You're a curious lady, aren't you?"

My cheeks flared. "Sorry, I didn't mean to be rude."

"I'm forty-six," she replied, then placed her clipboard on a table as we reached the front lobby.

"Do you have a family?"

She paused mid-step. Her gaze dropped. A silence carved into the air.

"Never mind. That was rude of me."

She met my eyes—for just a second.

"I think your friends came to pick you up. Goodbye, Alice."

She smiled, but the glow I remembered wasn't there. It felt like a goodbye forged from heartbreak. I hugged her. She didn't hug back. I waved and walked outside.

The moist air wrapped around me. I winced. A huge jeep, army print, no roof or windows, stood like a relic of chaos.

Leaning against it—the blonde girl I'd met on day one.

"How do you feel?" she asked, arms folded, calm but warm.

"I'm feeling better… thanks," I said softly, guilt nibbling at me for not knowing her better.

I slid into the back beside a girl with pale skin, bright orange hair, freckles, and piercing crystal blue eyes. She wore a cast on her left arm.

"I'm Stella! Your hair is so pretty," she said, touching it with watermelon-sweet breath.

"You're welcome for saving your life." Another girl, Ruby, chimed in from the front seat, feet propped up.

"She's very grumpy," Stella whispered, teasing.

"Am not! You're just annoying!"

"You see? Look how she treats me!" Stella laughed. I smiled—and this time, it wasn't forced.

"Clown," Ruby muttered. She wore a baggy black shirt and a camo cap pulled low.

"Well, jokes on all of you—I met Alice first. Day one, remember?" Naomi, the blonde, turned for a glance, then kept her eyes on the road.

"You showed me where my uniform was," I said, not meeting her gaze.

"Okay, Naomi, don't brag," Ruby mumbled.

"Guys, we're five minutes away."

"You all always fight like this?" I asked, shifting in the leather seat.

"Oh, you have no idea," Ruby said. "Especially those two." She looked thoughtful for a moment, then leaned in.

"Oh yeah… Alice, beware of Naomi's soaps. Don't borrow them. She'll freak."

Naomi shoved Ruby playfully. The jeep hit a bump. We all laughed.

When we arrived, the first thing I saw was Chief's scowl. I mimicked the salute, trying to look confident.

The base looked smaller than I remembered. Brighter. The air too still. Maybe it was the meds. Or maybe getting shot changes how you see the world.

Chief didn't smile. Just nodded. The kind of nod that said *this isn't a reunion.*

"You're walking better than expected," he said.

"Pain's not the worst thing I've felt," I replied, toughening my voice.

He didn't respond. Just turned and walked toward a building. I followed. The silence echoed.

Halfway down the hall, I stopped.

"Okay. What's going on?"

He turned slowly. His eyes looked... tired.

"You keeping me in captivity again?" I joked weakly.

"No. I'm not here to punish you."

He paused, then gestured to a seat. I sat down.

"As Chief, I need background on my soldiers."

"What do you mean, 'background'?"

"I know your history. Your family. Your education. Your whole life."

He stared at the floor.

"When did you find out? And why didn't you ever tell me?" My voice cracked—then rose.

"I understand your concern, Ms. Tillen…"

"Wait. What do you mean, 'Ms. Tillen'? What are you saying?" My chest tightened. My breath faltered. "Chief… what are you saying?"

Tears stung my eyes. *Hold them in. Hold them in. Hold them in.*

"With DNA testing," he continued, "we learned you're Herdonian. And… from the Tillen family." He hesitated. "We're not certain. But your parents may still be alive."

His sincerity rattled me.

"I need to leave. Excuse me."

I ran.

The sun beat down. My knees buckled. I fell into the sand. *Why today. Why this day. The day I get discharged—I get slapped in the face.*

Sweat poured. Tears fought through. *Hold them in. Hold them in. Please, Alice…*

"Alice?"

Joseph.

I wanted to say thank you. For everything. But the words disappeared.

"Go away, Joseph. Please." I couldn't fake strength anymore.

"What happened?" he asked, sitting in the burning sand.

"I need to leave, Joseph. Grab my stuff."

"What? Are you insane?"

"Joseph, please!"

"Not until you tell me what happened. Why are you about to cry?"

I met his eyes. Finally. And I whispered,

"I don't even know who I am anymore, Joseph. And I need to figure that out somewhere else."

He was stunned.

"You worked so hard to get here," he said. "Don't go. You have family—"

"What family, Joseph? *What family?*"

He dropped his gaze.

"There's something I need to tell you." I looked up.

"Chief's making his final decision tomorrow. Only three soldiers will stay. The rest... sent back."

"So soon?"

He nodded.

My lips pressed into a hard line.

I ran. Again. Everything inside me screamed.

The base door swung open.

"Hey Alice! Are you good?" Stella. Concern on her face.

I didn't answer. I couldn't.

They're safe. They won't be sent back. They were always part of this. I was just passing through.

I stepped past her. Into the bathroom.

Slam.

The room trembled.

Chapter XIII

"If you change the way you look at things, the things you look at change"-Wayne Dyer

My roommates stood clustered at the doorway, confusion etched into their faces.

"Why are you so annoyed?" Naomi's glare pierced through me.

I pushed past them, but Ruby blocked the exit.

"Move, Ruby," I said, avoiding her eyes.

"Uh uh, nope. Not letting you out until you talk."

"Move." I shoved her aside and slammed the heavy door behind me. I'd missed training yesterday. No excuses now.

Gun off my strap, body locked in place, I bolted across the yard. Soldiers stood in formation. Chief paced ahead, whispering with commanders.

I joined the line, spine straight, arm raised in salute.

"Go home," he said to one girl. She walked away crying.

"You…" Chief turned to Joseph. "Can stay." He nodded at another boy: "Go home." One at a time. Only three spots. *Go home. Go home. Go home,* my brain echoed.

"Alice," Chief paused. "You can stay."

Me? He said I could stay. The others were gone—sent back. Connor stood off to the side, surrounded by commanders. His golden hair fell across his eyes. Chief patted his shoulder, grinning.

"Genius! The boy's a genius!" He waved a paper in the air, covered in scribbles and dots.

"Walking drill!" The announcement sliced the air.

Jeep engines rumbled. I groaned. Walking drills were torture.

"Alice! Alice—wait!" Connor jumped onto my back.

"I got in! They said yes!" He beamed at me, pure joy pouring from his grin.

"Connor, that's great."

"You got in too?" I nodded, unsure whether it was relief or regret.

"Alice? You're in?" Joseph. Of course.

I looked away, my back burning. "Yes, I got in." Cold voice. No warmth.

Joseph turned to admire the view. Desert stretching endlessly.

"Joseph, is my hat straight?" A boy beside him turned and nodded.

"Yeah, it's fine." He clapped Joseph's shoulder. "Henry," he said, introducing his friend.

"What?" I asked.

"His name's Henry. He's a vibe." Joseph grinned.

"Okay…" I mumbled.

The jeep stopped hard. I almost slammed into the front seat. We climbed out, blistering sun attacking my skin.

"Why is it so hot?" Joseph fanned himself with his hat.

"Because it's a desert." I trudged west, sweat slipping down my face. Joseph fiddled with his compass, flipping it uselessly.

"How do you use this thing?"

I ignored him. Then—a noise.

"Alice—"

"Shh! Get down." I crouched low, ears trained.

"Alice, what are you—"

"JOSEPH, NO!" I tackled him just in time. A bullet sliced through the air beside us.

I raised my gun and fired. Neck. Stomach. Legs. The masked man collapsed.

I approached, checked for movement. Dead.

"You're lucky I'm here."

Joseph nodded, pale and shaken.

I grabbed the man's weapon, then turned to Joseph. "Do you know a shortcut back?"

"I've heard about bypasses… ones Chief doesn't even know."

I handed him his gun.

"If you want to be useful, lead me there."

"And what's the magic word?"

"Now!"

He muttered under his breath, then took the compass from my hand. "I don't know how to use this, but we should head north."

I yanked it back from him. When I was little, digging through junk in the basement, I found a compass. I taught myself how to use it. I taught myself how to escape.

Now the sun smacked me full in the face. But I walked. Walked until we reached the base.

Chapter XIV

"Think left and think right and think low and think high. Oh, the thinks you can think up if only you try!"-Dr. Seuss

My hat doubled as a fan. The sun fried my eyes, scorching everything in its path. I squinted, sure base A was just a few inches away.

"*Alice... I can't do this no more,*" Joseph gasped, swallowing air like it was rationed.

"There." I lifted my arm slowly, pointing forward. Then let it drop like a broken wing.

"Where?"

"I—I see the base," I choked out, dragging my body toward it. Noise behind me made me turn. Sun-blind as I was, I recognized that face. Henry.

"Joseph! What happened to you?" No exaggeration—Joseph looked like he'd lost a fight to five moving vehicles.

"Go away, Henry." Joseph waved his hand lazily in front of Henry's face. I paused, my body moving like a penguin trapped in glue.

"Please, *please* tell me there's a jeep five feet away from us!"

Henry stared, baffled. "Not you too. You know there's an easier way to get to base? Who told you to take the scenic route?"

My face flushed, cheeks radiating more heat than the desert.

"There was a shorter way…"

Joseph stepped back, defensive. "Hey—how was I supposed to know? At least we got our steps in."

I tackled him.

"You said you knew a shorter way!"

"Woah! Easy!" Henry pried me off Joseph as I thrashed.

"I HATE YOU—"

Henry clamped a hand over my mouth before I could finish. I pushed him off and stumbled forward, shoving past them with the last energy I had.

"Hey! Wait up!" Joseph trudged after me.

"What do you *want?*"

I stormed toward the language building. Chief's latest brilliant idea: Valkros language classes to understand our supposed enemies.

"Where are you going? Come on—it was an accident!"

"Why didn't we just stay with Henry?"

"You didn't want to work as a team."

I groaned. Our boots carved identical paths through the sand, but I kept my head low. Too many lies. Too much history. And the news I got after being discharged from the hospital—it still clawed at me.

"You gonna tell me where you're going?"

"Language, idiot. We're in the same class."

Every step ground sand into my aching legs. I didn't like this class. I didn't like much of anything anymore. But language, apparently, was our ticket to survival.

Mrs. Annabel was kind, impossibly patient. Even when it took a hundred attempts to pronounce *watch out,* she never raised her voice.

The door opened to air conditioning—pure heaven. Mrs. Annabel stood in her floral-patterned outfit, her warm brown eyes catching light like mystery.

"Lumiya, Mrs. Annabel," I greeted. I'd spent the whole night practicing how to say "hello."

"Lumiya, Alice. Today's lesson is emergency callouts—a review from last time."

Her accent rolled like silk. Everyone around here seemed to have accents that belonged in films.

"Lumiya, Joseph. Where were you last class?" Joseph blushed.

"I... hung out with friends."

I rolled my eyes and wiped sweat from my forehead.

The door slammed open.

"Hi, Joseph!"

"Connor!" Joseph jumped up and hugged his brother, joy lighting his exhausted face. Connor always smiled like he knew secrets that made life better. For a moment, I wished I had a brother too.

Soldiers filed in.

"Please take the sheet on my desk—we'll begin."

Mrs. Annabel spoke gently. "You've learned hello and goodbye. Now, let's work on 'help' and 'over here.'"

I looked down at the sheet. Valkros had one of the hardest languages ever. The first word made my brain stall.

"Next to number one, write *help,*" she said. Joseph leaned toward Connor and whispered something. Connor threw a pencil at his face.

"It was a joke! Calm down—"

"Boys." Mrs. Annabel's voice sharpened. Her stern gaze turned the room into stone.

"Joseph, no more bothering your brother. Understood?"

"Yes, ma'am…"

"Complete the rest of the pages using the notes above."

My handwriting was a disaster. I'd never gone to school. My stepmother said, *Books are enough.*

Mrs. Annabel clapped twice.

"You're scheduled to travel to Valkros on Monday. Study this vocabulary. Am I clear?"

Clear? I was going to die. Get shot. Perish. Maybe even get punched to death.

But what could I say?

War is a filthy game.

Chapter XV

"Everyone should be respected as an individual, but no one idolized"-Albert Einstein

Language class was dull as ever, and my roommates made it worse. As I walked into the base, a shoe whipped past my face.

"What is *wrong* with you guys!" I snapped.

"Oh! I'm so sorry!" Ruby popped out of her ridiculous hiding spot, hands raised like she wasn't guilty. "I thought you were Naomi."

I glared, shut the door behind me.

"But now that you're here..." she smirked. "You can *finally* tell us why you were so mean earlier."

Her smile had the kind of smug curve that made me want to slap it off.

"Come on. Tell us—"

"Go away."

I tossed my dirty clothes to the side and climbed into my bunk. Arms under my head. Legs crossed. I felt disgusting, sweat sticking to me like glue, but too drained to shower.

Their whispers drilled into me. So did their eyes.

But all I could think of was my parents.

What I'd give—just one minute. One hug. One hello.

I couldn't remember if I'd cried when Joseph convinced me to stay. Maybe I had. But I was numb now. Sadness blurred into static. Still, the lump in my throat was growing, pressing, waiting.

Hold it in. Hold it in. Hold it in.

The ceiling reminded me of my old room. Rusty. Bare. Ugly in a familiar way.

The roommates kept cycling moods—silence, chaos, gossip. I tracked them with my eyes as they packed up for dinner.

I hadn't moved.

"Are you coming with us? Or still mad?" Naomi asked.

"Naomi, stop. You're annoying her," Stella said. "I'll wait for Alice."

Naomi was hard work. But she held this fractured group together better than anyone.

The door slammed shut behind them.

Stella stayed, back against the pole of her bunk. Arms and legs folded like locked doors. Head tipped toward the floor.

I sat up.

"You ready to go?" she asked softly.

I didn't answer.

"Not to be annoying," she continued, "but you *need* to talk to someone."

I fiddled with the front pocket of my pants.

"Why should I?"

She climbed up to sit across from me on my bunk, eyes steady.

"Because you're turning into Naomi when she's mad—and that's terrifying."

I tilted my head to the side, chin resting on my shoulder.

"My parents…"

They're gone. Always gone. I never even had a chance.

"They left me when I was little."

The lump came back—huge and full of pressure. Like the tears were fists, punching their way up.

Shed one, Alice. Just one. What's it going to cost you?

"Chief says they could still be alive."

Stella's hand flew to her chest. The other covered her mouth.

"Isn't that good news?"

"No." My voice went sharp, wrapped in hurt. "Not if someone else knows more about my family than I do."

I stood, walked to the door.

"I'm going to eat."

Her eyes followed me, wide with empathy, still seated on my bunk as I disappeared.

Chapter XVI

"Your attitude, not your aptitude, will determine your altitude"-Zig Ziglar

The cafeteria was warm. The smell of sauce drifted into my nose—reminding me of home. Not the cozy kind. The kind of home where I was treated like I never belonged. Where my bed felt like a rugged mountain smothering a prairie.

Part of me wondered: were they angry I left? Sad? Happy?

My eyes landed on Connor in the far corner, seated with Joseph and a few others. I dragged myself toward their table.

"Hey A, did you calm down earlier?" My hands trembled. I wanted to punch his stupid, smug, pathetic face.

"Why are you guys standing?" My voice barely carried over the chaos around us.

"We have to," Henry said.

I slid into place—Naomi to my right, Stella on my left, Joseph and Connor across the long table. My fingers brushed the Polaroid in my pocket.

I stared ahead, waiting for food, but all I heard above the clatter was our table. Naomi launched into a story.

"Henry, didn't you lock yourself in your room as a kid to practice singing—" He cut her off.

"Didn't you wet the bed 'til you were *eleven*?"

The table exploded in laughter. Naomi flushed behind her tan cheeks.

"You two are siblings?" I asked.

"Yeah. Hard to tell, since one of us clearly looks better," Henry teased. Naomi coughed and dramatically said her name under her breath.

"What are *your* siblings like, Alice?" Naomi asked.

Panic prickled my spine.

"I'm an only child." Not technically a lie. Not technically the truth.

I glanced at Stella. Her smile was soft—almost sad.

"Makes sense," she said.

"What's *that* supposed to mean?"

"Nothing," she muttered, glancing at Henry. His blond hair—same shade as Naomi's—caught the light like it was designed to be noticed. Bright. Blinding.

A tall woman with pale skin arrived at our table carrying trays of salad and pasta. I reached for a plate just as Joseph started serving himself.

"Wait! You can't eat now!" Henry hissed, yanking the plate from Joseph's hands.

"What? Why not?" Joseph tried to grab it back, but Henry dumped the food back into the bowl.

Confused, I gently asked Naomi, "Why can't we eat?"

She smiled. "Chief trains us with temptation. We stand in front of food and don't touch it. Eat even one piece... it's jail time. Like what happened to you."

My eyes widened. "How do you know it was *me*?"

"Word spreads quickly."

Henry grinned. "You're sleeping on the floor this time, just so you know."

"You had the bed last time. We switch, Henry—I *called* my room earlier this week, remember?"

"You're so annoying. Always hogging."

"Henry, *please*, you had your room last weekend!" They argued like toddlers fighting over chocolate. My stomach growled. Steam from the pasta taunted me.

"You have family in Herdonia?" Joseph asked.

I blinked.

"No. Why?"

"Where do you stay on weekends?"

"At my base."

"Most take weekend shifts *unless* needed," he said, arms crossed.

I noticed Connor whispering to Joseph.

"No, Connor. Auntie won't let us," Joseph replied.

"I think it's a great idea!" Connor chirped. "Alice, stay at Auntie's—there's a spare room!"

I cut him off before he could offer me more.

"Connor… it's fine. I'll stay here. Like always."

I tried to sound humble. But Connor's frown was the only thing I saw.

"Shh! We can't talk anymore!" Naomi whispered just as Chief's voice drowned everyone.

"Not one sound! Look at your food!"

We stared.

I glanced at Ruby. She didn't blink. She didn't flinch. Poker face.

I thought about staying with Joseph's family. Staying here meant more work. More isolation. But disrupting their life… no thanks.

The salad was vibrant—tomatoes, cucumbers, spinach. Cut too perfectly. Like someone *wanted* us to suffer.

One hour passed. Then two. Almost three.

Chief finally said we could eat.

"Gosh, I thought I was about to cry," Henry groaned, scooping pasta like a pro.

"Leave some for *me!*" Connor shoved him. Joseph joined in, wrestling for a scoop. I filled my plate—pasta, salad, everything. I ate like I hadn't in years. It was *divine.* Bite after bite. Gone. I looked up—everyone else was still eating. My face flushed pink.

Stella caught my eye. Her smile was quiet. Compassionate.

One by one, plates emptied. People cleaned up.

I slipped away, my tray in hand—quiet as a shadow.

Chapter XVII

"No act of kindness, no matter how small, is ever wasted"-
Aesop

I sat on my bed, eyes fixed on the ceiling. It was my favorite place to look—so much space for thoughts to drift. I thought of Lia. Of everything unsaid.

"Hey Alice, you left early," Naomi said as she and the others stepped in, heading for their beds.

"I was tired," I lied. Truth was, I could've stayed up all night fighting, waiting, crying.

"I'm going to shower," Naomi announced, scooping up her clothes.

"We won't steal your soaps!" Ruby howled, rolling on her bed.

"Quit it!" Naomi shouted from behind the door.

I hissed in pain. My back. It seized up—sharp, burning. A familiar agony, like I was getting shot all over again. The fire crept lower, radiating through my spine.

"You okay?" Stella jumped off her bed.

"My back… I can't move!" I choked on the words, trying to hold back tears.

"Ruby—tell Naomi we left for the hospital!" Ruby nodded as Stella swept me into her arms.

She laid me gently in the jeep's leather seat and drove fast—too fast. I squeezed my eyes shut.

The hospital loomed large ahead. Inside, I was placed on a bed. Everything was noise. Not the soft hum of people. Buzzing. Static.

"Please help!" Stella begged. "She was just discharged from a severe gunshot—her back hurts and she can't move!"

My body ached. My ears rang. Every sound melted into a dull hum. Everything blurred... except the orange of Stella's hair disappearing down the hallway.

Then, blackness.

Chapter XVIII

"There is nothing impossible to him who will try"-Alexander the Great

I woke with something pressing against my nose. A tube. Helping me breathe. My vision was blurry. I was back in the same hospital room where it all began.

"Alice, honey. How are you feeling?" Lia sat beside me. Her glass-green eyes—soft, elegant—reflected the sterile light.

"What's wrong with my back?" My voice was fragile. Barely mine.

"Some patients react to surgery like this. Yours... it was more extreme." Her voice danced gently through the air, threaded with a distant accent. "You'll return to training when you're ready, but on the battlefield, you'll need to be careful. Too much strain... and it could leave you paralyzed. Permanently."

I wanted to sob. Scream. Empty the pain I'd tucked away for no one to see.

"I want to go home. I shouldn't have come here." Each word cracked as it left my throat.

Lia sighed, eyes drifting to the window.

"Alice... your family lives far away. You know you can't do that."

She placed her files neatly on the bedside table.

"What's your family like?" I asked.

She hesitated, leaned her head into her hand.

"I had a husband. A beautiful little girl…" She stopped. "I had to leave her behind. Needed time to get through my life I guess."

Tears blurred her polished composure. I lowered my gaze, giving her space. Waiting.

"I'm sorry," she whispered, wiping tears before they fell.

I tucked my blanket closer. "I wasn't too lucky with family either."

She tilted her head.

"But your file says you're part of a family of five."

I'd forgotten—most people knew nothing about my real past.

"I don't want to get into it." I swallowed. "But I had a story like yours… except…" A pause. "I was the child left behind."

Silence.

My hands ached. I stared at them. At how small they felt. Lia opened her mouth, but another doctor entered quietly.

"Lia, Jill is waiting in room seventeen." He vanished, leaving the door ajar.

"I have to go," Lia said. "You'll get your medicine at base—one dose daily."

She stood, graceful as ever. Before walking out, she turned. Her eyes met mine. A gentle smile flickered across her lips.

Then she was gone.

Chapter XIX

"Every story I create, creates me. I write to create myself"-
Octavia E. Butler

A soft pink gummy sat between my fingers. It didn't
look appetizing. I started to put it back when a hand stopped
me.

"Oh no you don't!" Stella snatched the container and
dropped the gummy into her palm. "You *have* to eat it." She
grabbed her gear while I shoved the gummy into my mouth.

"That is *horrible!*" I gagged, wincing.

Stella laughed and tossed me my gun. "It's a
painkiller. Now let's go." She skipped out. I struggled to
swallow. Outside, the desert greeted me like a curse. The heat
clung to my skin. My boots sank into the sand.

"Alice!" It was Joseph, waving from another group
beside Connor.

"You can join us—it's starting!" I headed toward
them, but Chief's eyes locked on me. Worried. Suspicious.

"What are we doing?" I asked him.

"Running," he replied, grinning sharply.

I followed the group's rhythm. My steps fell into sync.
It had been nearly six weeks since I left home. The desert heat
was habit now. But my heart wasn't soothed. Monday was
coming—battle was coming.

"Joseph?" I panted.

"Hm?"

"Are you scared?"

He watched his feet. Then looked up.

"It's risky. But I think we'll make it." A sly grin flickered over his uncertainty.

"Tag!" He bolted forward.

"Hey!" I shouted, chasing him through sand and sun. My boots kicked up dust. The uniform clung. I couldn't stop.

Joseph slowed. I didn't.

"Tag!" I struck his shoulder.

He gasped and collapsed, face-first.

I burst into laughter, watching clouds drift overhead. Connor pulled him up and dashed to my side.

"Alice!" His smile was sunshine.

"Hey buddy." I placed a hand on his shoulder.

"I called Auntie—you know what she said?"

"What?"

"You can stay with us this weekend!" I froze. My heart skipped.

"Oh, Connor… I really don't need to." I scraped together excuses. Training. Focus. Space.

Joseph caught up.

"She said it's *fine,* Alice," Connor pressed, tugging Joseph's hand.

Joseph looked at me like the choice was mine.

"I don't want to bother your aunt—"

"You won't," Joseph said gently.

I glanced at the group approaching.

"Well... if it really doesn't bother her... then sure."

I gave a crooked smile. Gratitude tucked behind nerves. They felt like a new kind of family.

"Yay!" Connor beamed. "We've got a spare room!"

We jogged together. Sand heavy beneath our feet. I turned to Joseph.

"What's it like growing up with Connor?"

He didn't hesitate.

"It's the best thing that ever happened to me. His disability? It didn't feel like it existed." He paused. Envy shadowed his tan face. "I still get jealous—he's so damn smart."

I smiled, then ran. Fast. Free. My feet ached, but training had taught me how to push past pain.

As we neared base, Chief spoke with two figures. I ran closer.

No. It was her.

Stepmother. And him. My grumpy, stone-faced stepfather. Their faces folded in familiar scorn.

Stepmother's eyes caught mine.

"Good lord! Alice?" she gasped.

I froze. Her face hadn't changed. But mine had.

"You are *coming home,* now!"

She stormed toward me. I stepped back.

"Alice," Chief said, "Do you want to go with this woman?"

I shook my head. Quiet. Resolute.

"No. Not at all, Sir."

"Very well. We no longer need your presence, Mr. and Mrs. Rogers."

"We're not leaving!" she barked. Then with a sneer, she pulled a crumpled envelope from her purse and slammed it into my hand.

"*Peter wanted you to have this,*" she spat. "Don't know why. Waste of ink if you ask me."

Before I could answer, she grabbed my arm. I hit the sand hard. Pain surged across my cheek.

Chief didn't flinch. Two generals appeared and escorted them away.

I watched as my past vanished into the desert. Two shadows swallowed by heat and silence.

I nodded at Chief.

He returned the gesture—then turned back to training.

Later that night, I sat by a window near my bed and pulled out the envelope. Peter's handwriting was shaky—but familiar.

Dear Alice,

I don't expect you to answer. Probably not even to read this.

Stepmother said you left without a word. That you didn't care. I know better, but it still stings.

You never said goodbye. Not to me. Not to the garden. I've been working the soil alone since you vanished, and it doesn't feel right.

Things back home are as cold as ever. Your stepmother pretends she's relieved. But she still curses every time she walks past your door. Your stepfather calls you "ungrateful," like he ever offered anything worth being grateful for.

You used to sit by the azaleas when you were too sad to cry. I keep checking there, half-hoping you'll be back with that distant look in your eyes. But I'm starting to think the silence is permanent.

My mother passed away. I couldn't save her, Alice.

Still... I don't blame you. You made a choice to survive, and I respect that—even if it hurt.

Don't come back for us. But come back for yourself, someday. Or at least let someone know you're okay.

You mattered to me, Alice. Way more than they ever knew.

—Peter Nobal

Chapter XX

"Whoever is happy will make others happy too"-Anne Frank

Last night, I took the bus with Joseph and Connor, and woke up in a huge bed where large, modern windows flooded my eyes with sunlight. Joseph's aunt's place was enormous. Almost like a castle.

I got out of bed and headed to my bathroom. My very own bathroom. I used to think having a roof over my head and food on the table meant living like royalty—but this place made me rethink everything. I brushed my teeth with the mint toothpaste neatly placed next to the bar of soap. The only problem was that I didn't have any proper clothes, apart from the ones I left home with. They didn't smell the best: old, crusty hoodies that had been sitting in my closet for years.

I pulled on my black running tank top and the pants from my uniform. Then I replaced those with a pair of baggy jeans I found in one of the drawers and a snug navy-blue shirt.

I quickly brushed my hair and tied it into a messy ponytail. I was tanner than when I first arrived, and tiny freckles had appeared on my nose from the sun. I liked them.

They made me feel pretty. I opened the beautiful white doors leading out of my bedroom and somehow found my way to the kitchen.

"Good morning, Ms. Berg," I beamed as she placed a plate on the long marble counter, which glowed in the morning sun.

"Good morning, Alice. I made you some breakfast," she said, tilting her head toward the plate—scrambled eggs, sliced fruits and vegetables, and a red apple. I stared at the apple, remembering eating one on the streets. The boy. The boy. He saved me from hunger.

"You made me breakfast?" I asked, stunned, keeping my distance from the table.

"Well, yes. Come sit and enjoy, sweetheart," she said, walking to the chair and pulling it out for me.

"Why didn't you let me make my own breakfast?"

"I know you must be tired. It's the least I can do, especially since you have a big day on Monday." I stared at her vaguely. No one had ever made breakfast just for me. Back at base, we made our own meals, and the food was bland compared to what I was seeing now.

"Thank you," I said steadily as I sat down, letting the sweet scent of my breakfast wash over me.

"Well now, enjoy! I need to wake the boys. They never get up as early as you do, dear. It's almost six-thirty!"

"I guess I'm a morning person," I said with a wide smile, tilting my head to my shoulder.

"You and I are very similar, I can tell! Oh—and I also have a separate training room you can use."

She walked away, leaving me flabbergasted.

Ms. Berg was rich.

I ate my breakfast like a pig. I appreciated the food served to me far more than what I used to make for myself—

meals that barely filled me up. All that remained on the plate were a few pieces of spinach and the red apple. I picked it up and held it close to my eyes. Then I took a bite.

Fourteen years ago. The streets were busy, as they always were on a Wednesday morning. I sat next to a dumpster in the crevice between two brick walls, watching important people walk by. I never begged for money. Even at three years old, I knew the difference between earned and stolen.

One thing I always expected was the boy with blue eyes bringing me an apple every day when the restaurant clock across the street struck eleven.

"I hope it's enough for you," his tiny voice had said.

To this day, I wonder who that boy was. I remember him being close to my age.

"Morning, Alice!" I turned around to see Connor in dinosaur pajamas, full of energy.

"Morning," I said, flashing a tired smile as I headed to wash my dirty dishes. Joseph followed, wearing a white shirt with gingham pants. I scrubbed the last dish and started to dry it.

"Why are you cleaning the dishes?" Joseph rubbed his eyes and sat down next to Connor.

"Am I not supposed to?" I stopped moving the towel across the plate.

"Oh no, you're allowed—but we have a dishwasher. You don't need to do it by hand." My eyes widened.

"I'm allowed to use your dishwasher?" Joseph looked confused by my excitement.

"Yeah, I guess," he shrugged, pointing toward it. I skipped over happily.

"Why are you so happy about a dishwasher?" I didn't want to explain the years I'd spent scrubbing dishes with soap that made my nails brittle.

"It's nothing. Hurry and eat. We don't have all day," I said, waving my hand dismissively.

"I don't like being rushed," Joseph said, rolling his eyes and taking a bite of breakfast.

"Sorry, *Prince*. You should've woken up earlier." I left the kitchen before more chatter could unfold.

My old socks slid across the bright white marble. The gym was magnificent.

Tall windows lined the walls, embracing the modern design, with all the training equipment neatly laid out. To my right, glass doors revealed a long, clean pool. I slowly placed my hands on a metal bar attached to the wall.

Connor and Joseph had everything they needed to live happily and healthily. That thought made me uneasy. I'd always been jealous of people like them. I walked over to a corner where a few jump ropes caught my eye. I grabbed one, slipped off my socks, and let the cold marble floor meet my feet. Then I jumped.

Fourteen, fifteen, sixteen hops. My heartbeat quickened. My feet slipped. I refocused and jumped faster.

I noticed the wide open gym doors just as Connor walked in.

"Hello," I greeted him weakly, nearly gasping. Connor gave me one of his jubilant smiles—the kind that wouldn't hurt a fly. I hoped that smile wouldn't disappear after Monday.

He hopped up on a chair. A desk mounted to the wall held a computer and a black mouse. I kept jumping, heart pounding. I watched Connor scribble long paragraphs on paper.

Sudden footsteps startled me.

"Connor, what's that?" Joseph ran his fingers through his wavy hair.

"They gave me homework!" Connor groaned, resting his head in his hand. His smile was gone. I stopped jumping, feeling sick.

"I don't think we should train after we eat," I said, covering my mouth to keep from throwing up.

"Nah, you'll get used to it," Joseph said, grabbing a mat and laying it flat on the floor. I placed my sweaty palms on a nearby bar and pulled myself up.

One rep. My arms dropped.

Another lift. My chin grazed the bar. Third rep. My hand slipped—I clung tighter.

I let go, arms trembling.

"Already tired?" Joseph teased.

I glared at him. "Pardon?" I said, walking past him toward the pool. The sun sparkled on the water.

"Ninety-two!" "Ninety-three!" "Ninety-four!"

"Quit counting so loud!" I shouted, fists clenched as I tilted my head toward the ceiling. My ears felt like they were ringing.

"Yeah, you're so annoying!" Connor jumped off the chair and kicked Joseph in the stomach, walking away without hesitation. Joseph groaned and continued doing push-ups.

Connor skipped back to the desk, resuming his writing.

What was he working on? Why did they give him homework on the weekend?

Chapter XXI

"Opportunities are usually disguised as hard work, so most people don't recognize them"-Ann Landers

It was almost nine, and I had just gotten out of the pool. I swam in sweaty clothes. My shirt clung to my skin. It didn't feel pleasant. I was tired and no longer wanted to train.

Joseph dried his hair with a towel, and Connor did the same.

"We've got a couple more laps around the backyard," Joseph said, tossing his towel onto a chair.

"Tomorrow," I whispered. I didn't want to train anymore. Monday was getting closer, and I was growing more and more nervous.

"What do you mean, tomorrow?" He sounded irritated by my fatigued and weak response.

"I don't feel like training," I said, throwing my towel aside and walking awkwardly as my wet clothes dragged behind me.

"Alice! We leave in one day!" His voice grated on me. It carried frustration, maybe even fear.

"One full day to train," I replied, walking slowly.

"What's wrong with you? What if Valkros attacks our neighborhood tomorrow?" He was yelling now, and I realized I'd never seen him this angry. I wasn't scared—I was astonished.

"They won't… I'm going to sleep." I stepped into the cold gym.

"Alice, you've suffered too much to give up now. Please. We have one day." I felt him behind me. His anger thickened the air. I stopped walking and spun around to face both Connor and an agitated Joseph. His words echoed: *You've lost and suffered so much to give up now.*

"Joseph, what do you mean I've lost and suffered so much?" He couldn't have known. He shouldn't have known.

"Nothing. Let's go. We've got laps to do." I stepped in, cutting him off.

"No—it is something. What do you know about me, Joseph?" Connor's expression shifted.

"Alice, I care about you. I notice when you're sad and trying to hide it. I see every emotion. You really think you can keep that from me?"

We walked outside just as the sun started to set. Sweat poured down my face.

Connor tugged at Joseph's sleeve, mouthing "no." He knew the lines—not because of his diagnosis, but because Connor always knew what was right… and what wasn't.

"Never mind. We have to hurry—it's almost sundown." Connor ran for the orange cones by the pool and set them across the long field of grass. I gave in, setting myself in a rest position, ready to run. My legs were shaking from the training earlier, but I pushed forward. The pain was unbearable. My muscles screamed beneath my skin. Still, I kept running.

Sweat streamed from my face, caught in the breeze as the wind pushed against me. Ms. Berg's backyard was bigger than my stepparents' entire house.

One lap. Another. Third. Fourth.

I was close to quitting. My back throbbed—shouting, *stop. Wake up. This is all a dream.*

My last lap.

I was terrified that I'd wake up in that same old, shabby basement—cold and dry with dust falling into my hair. That I'd be forced to make breakfast for everyone, get yelled at anyway. That I'd be hiding bruises again with fresh packs of foundation.

I was scared I'd see Ford and Dixie driving off to school… while I stayed behind. I remembered sneaking books just to teach myself every night. No one taught me to read.

Or to solve math problems. Or to sing. Or play violin. Or write.

Now I realize—no one taught me anything.

We walked inside together—Connor and Joseph laughing, while I silently wondered: Will I ever meet even *one* of my parents?

It wasn't fair.

Two brothers in a house like this… a private gym, a private pool, a private backyard.

I found my way to my room.

"Night, Alice," Connor said, waving with his shaky hand before disappearing into his own room.

Joseph turned to me. "Night. Also, my aunt wanted me to tell you she left some clothes in your room for tomorrow." He waved and headed to the room next to mine.

"Goodnight," I said softly.

Chapter XXII

"Walking with a friend in the dark is better than walking alone in the light"-Helen Keller

The sun struck my face through the window as I dressed. Ms. Berg had filled my drawers with expensive-looking hoodies and designer pants, but I chose the simplest: a black shirt and grey shorts. I didn't want comfort to come from price tags.

Near my bed, worn-out shoes rested quietly beside gleaming new runners. Engraved designs danced along their sides. I slid my foot into one—they were a bit big, but cloud-soft. I jogged in place. It felt incredible.

Downstairs, breakfast was waiting. Ms. Berg waved from behind the counter.

"Good morning, honey. How are you feeling?"

"A bit sore, but okay." I perched on the stool. "Thanks for the clothes and shoes. I really appreciate them. I just don't know how to repay you."

"You don't need to repay me," she said softly. "Take it as a gift."

"Are you sure?" I hesitated, nudging sliced strawberries on my plate.

"I'm more than positive. Now eat—tomorrow's a big day."

I gazed at her as she left the kitchen. Do people give gifts just because? The strawberry hit my sensitive tooth, and I grimaced.

After breakfast, I practiced sit-ups in the gym. Each rep peeled pain off my spine. I was halfway through when Connor's voice echoed. Milk mustache and all, he waved cheerily.

"Where… are you going?" he asked, twisting on his stool.

"Just grabbing something. I'll be back."

In my room, I downed the nasty pink gummy. Relief was instant.

Joseph was already downstairs. Two pairs of blue eyes met mine. He gave a lazy wave. I smiled through the pain and returned to the gym.

Rain tapped the windows. My mind drifted.

I remembered the car ride. Rain. A cold leather seat. My stepmother barking orders. Chores piled high. I'd watch raindrops race across glass just to escape reality. I was nine. Holding back tears. Always saving them for bedtime.

A hand waved near my face. Joseph, with a jump rope.

"Alice? You good?"

"Yeah. Yeah, I'm fine," I lied.

I laid back down. Four. Five. Six. I was grateful for the clothes. The soft fabric cradled my sweat.

"Thanks," I said mid-sit-up.

"Don't worry about it," Joseph replied, lowering onto a mat beside me.

One hundred sit-ups later, my heart was a drum. My pulse a battle cry. As they headed outside, I staggered to my feet.

I was thirteen. Staring into a cracked mirror. I tried to run away once. A duffel bag. A toothbrush. A stolen bag of chips. The alarm screamed. My stepparents stormed in—one with a clothing rack, the other with a metal bat.

"How dare you try to run away, Alice!"

"I wasn't going to run away. I was just taking out the trash." A lie. One of many.

Connor bounced with excitement. "We're going to the pool! Auntie said we can go for ice cream after!" I forced a smile. My eyes burned from crying.

Ms. Berg caught my tired stare.

"Already tired?" I couldn't respond. "Alice, is everything okay?" I shook my head. "Come sit." Her hand rested on my shoulder.

"Ms. Berg…" My voice shook. Hold in the tears. Hold them in. "I wasn't supposed to come here."

Her eyes softened. I told her everything—adoption, labor, fear of returning after the war.

She looked like she might shatter. "My poor child… Joseph told me he recognized you. Said he gave you apples in Nuvoria." I froze.

"What?"

"He wanted to tell you himself."

"How did he know?"

"Maybe you still carry pieces of that little girl in you." She smiled. "You're always welcome here."

"Thank you," I whispered. The tears were gone now.

"Tomorrow is a big day," she said, gripping my shoulders. Not just words—strength passed between us.

I walked to the bus station. My bag weighed me down, my gun strapped tightly. The sunset bled across the sky.

Connor and Joseph sat on the bench. I startled Connor when I dropped my bag too hard.

"I'm sorry." I adjusted myself.

"Alice?" Connor blinked at me with his baby-blue eyes.

"Yeah?"

"When we're in Valkros... do you pinky promise you won't let anybody shoot me?"

I paused.

"I pinky promise, Connor."

Chapter XXIII

"You only live once, but if you do it right, once is enough"-
Mae West

I gripped my hand on the jeep, praying my sweat would slide off. It was four A.M., and my pink chewy gummy was still filling my mouth with that awful flavor. We came to a sudden stop—my body lurched forward. We were hidden behind a wall of mountains. No light. No sound.

I took my gun off its strap and reloaded it. *Click.* The loudest sound in our group. My roommates were all nearby, joined last minute by Joseph's team.

"We don't have much time. A prisoner told command she was placed in a tall building. That's our first stop." Henry sounded serious—more serious than I'd ever seen him. Almost nervous. But not quite. He couldn't be.

"Alice and Connor, you'll enter through the back. Stay quiet. The rest of us will cover outside. Connor, you memorized the map?"

Connor nodded. I faked confidence. Always fake it.

We dropped to our stomachs and crawled across the sand, guns secure. I glanced right to make sure Connor was still beside me. His eyes were squeezed shut. Breath deep and shaky.

"You're going to be okay," I whispered, forcing a smile. Fake it. He looked at me—his big blue eyes no longer bright.

The building loomed ahead. We were here. I rose, then ducked low, hugging my gun. A nod from Henry. I returned it. Once. Quietly.

Connor and I moved toward the rear door. I raised my gun.

POP!

Stella cut across my path. "Herdonian army! Evacuate the premises now!" Her voice scorched the air. I stayed steady. Fake it.

Chaos erupted. Our team charged as bullets ripped through the dust. I grabbed Connor's arm and sprinted toward the building. Forget everything. My friends were outside, maybe bleeding. Maybe gone.

Three left turns, just like Connor said. We hit a long hallway lined with shelves of chicken cages. All empty. Until—

A cry. A baby.

First cage—nothing. Second—still nothing. Third—a baby. Tiny. Maybe two months old, wheezing for breath.

"Connor, keep watch." I lifted the baby gently from the cage.

"Take her. Joseph's waiting. Go!" Connor's shoes were soft against the concrete, barely audible.

I turned back to the hallway. Left. Right. Left again. Something was wrong.

Then I saw him.

A masked man. Only his eyes visible.

"Who are you?" My voice trembled. I raised my gun.

He shot first—missed. I didn't move. I studied my surroundings, repositioned, fired.

One hit. Then another.

He lunged. My body slammed against the wall. Blood poured from my arm.

Scream? No. Anger instead. Fake it.

I used my good arm, and somehow I had him under my possession.

He collapsed. I moved on. Hallway after hallway. Nothing but emptiness. My sleeve was soaked in blood, but I didn't stop.

Then—an open door. Darkness. Cold.

I stepped closer. *Drip... drip...* My blood echoed through the silence.

The wooden stairs groaned beneath me. Three steps left. My heart pounded. My eyes blurred. My cheeks burned.

A woman sat in the corner, curled around herself. Her face pale, her knees drawn to her chest.

"Ma'am, are you alone?" She looked up slowly. One nod. Then another.

I placed my gun aside, extended my good arm.

She didn't move.   I pointed to the Herdonian badge on my uniform. "Please. We don't have much time."

Her hand reached for mine. She was skeletal—fragile. I pulled her up, draped her arm over my shoulder, wrapped mine around her waist.

Ahead—the red EXIT sign.

I kicked the door. Sunlight blasted through. The desert of Valkros glared in our faces.

I limped toward the sand dune.

"My child," she whispered. "My child in a cage."

"We found your baby, ma'am," I said coldly. My body numb.

She blinked. Confused.

I hurried toward the others.

Joseph was lying beside Henry, his leg soaked in blood. The sand refused to absorb it.

"My G-d—Joseph?"

"Shot in the leg. Doesn't matter. Connor's in the tank with the baby. Take her."

I rushed. Connor cradled the baby—small, precious, finally breathing.

"Charlie!" The woman cried out, hobbling toward her child. Ruby followed, med kit in hand.

I ran again. Pain trailed behind me.

"Henry, we need to leave! They're everywhere!" My lungs burned. Fake it.

"You were shot?"

"Doesn't matter!" I waved toward the team. "We'll die if we stay!"

Henry looked to Joseph. He pulled his hat off, revealing a wound on his cheek, and nodded.

"Alice, your arm—you're losing too much blood."

"Later."

"You'll faint—"

"We don't have time!"

I grabbed the tank's pole and climbed aboard. Joseph collapsed into the last seat, his cast dragging.

The hatch sealed behind us. And we started to leave.

Chapter XXIV

"Never give a sword to a man who can't dance"-Confucius

Night was the only thing calling my name. The tips of the stars blinded my eyes as we settled into a small patch of sand. Some of us were healing. Others were silent and sleeping.

Henry murmured quietly with Joseph while Connor slowly dozed beside them, curled up like a child. I lay on the warm sand, clutching the thick cast Henry had wrapped around my arm. The pain was awful—something I was used to.

The woman rested with her baby nestled in her arms. Naomi passed her a blanket, one of few comforts we had left. I let my feet relax. Just once. Our first day in Valkros had been chaos—blood, shots in arms and legs, threats and sacrifices. I closed my eyes, and the memory returned.

Ford and Dixie on the swings. Stepmother and stepfather chatting on the porch. And across the street—there he was. A blond boy with blue eyes, handing out apples. Apples... the blond hair, the blue eyes.

I opened my eyes. No longer tired.

I pushed myself up with my free arm and turned to the left.

"Joseph," I hissed.

A shadow shifted in the distance. He limped toward me, sand whispering beneath his steps. He lowered himself to the ground, balancing with his arms.

"What's up?" He rubbed his injured leg slowly. I knew that pain.

"Where did you live before all of this?" My voice wasn't angry. Just sharp.

"Nuvoria. You know that."

"Where did you go in the mornings, when you were younger?"

"Shoot, that was ages ago, Alice... You think I remember all that?" He paused. "I used to walk with my mom to the corner store, I think." His voice wavered.

"Nothing else? Never gave apples to a homeless girl?" He froze. His hands stopped moving.

"Alice... I was going to tell you." His voice was low and hesitant. "It's not what you think."

"It isn't?"

"You can't be mad. I only recognized you recently."

"Quit it, Joseph! Why did you do all that for me? Why didn't you tell me the moment you knew? Why? Why? Why?" I strained to keep my voice low.

"Who told you?"

"That doesn't matter." "Did you know who I was back then?"

"I'd heard about you." I rolled my eyes.

"How much do you know?"

"Not much. So don't worry." He didn't sound defensive anymore. Just tired.

Morning came. Valkros didn't feel any less broken.

The woman still cradled her baby—fragile and pale. Naomi stayed close, soothing the infant who was breathing even worse than before. She deserved the credit. She had held that child together.

We packed our food. Guns were loaded. The air was tense.

"Joseph and Alice—you two stay here," Ruby said flatly.

My head snapped up.

"Why?" Was it my arm?

"You both need medical attention." She placed a basket of bread in the tank.

"No! Please! I'm fine. Really, I am!"

"Alice, keep your voice down." Stella placed a hand gently on my shoulder.

"Please," I begged. My voice cracked under control.

"No is no, Alice. Naomi will take you both to base."

I clenched my fists—pain screamed through my cast.

Chapter XXV

"There is nothing permanent except change"-Heraclitus

I got out of the tank with Joseph.

No.

All our bases—bombed.

No.

I wanted to scream. I needed to scream. NO!

Joseph was speechless, lips parted in shock. I gripped my gun tighter.

Then—an explosion burst in the distance. The hospital.

"NO!" I ran. I cried. "LIA!" My legs were swollen, shaking beneath me. But I ran.

Soldiers shouted, tried to stop me, tried to hold me back.

I ran faster.

A tank rolled toward the same destination, but I was already ahead.

I remembered—brief flashes.

A young woman holding me. I was just a baby. Her eyes—bright green. A lullaby in the blur of memory. Those green eyes—so beautiful.

It was her. Lia. My mother.

The hospital was gone.

I dropped to my knees. "LIA!" I cried until the sound broke me. I kept running.

The building was scorched. Bodies everywhere. Blood pooled thick like wine across cracked stone.

"NOO!" My scream broke the air. I had no voice left.

Soldiers hurried past me—lifting bodies, shouting orders, searching for survivors.

I ran anyway.

And then—I saw her.

Lia. Eyes wide open. Her arm rested on her stomach, unmoving. Blood spilled from her neck… her head.

Her legs—twisted, disfigured. It hurt to look.

"WHY? THIS ISN'T FAIR?" My tears, real ones, not the kind I taught myself to hide—poured down my cold, shivering face.

Joseph, Naomi, and other soldiers stood behind me, frozen.

A name tag glinted from her charred jacket. Lia Tillen.

No. She couldn't be. She mustn't be.

Lia was my mother.

I dropped to the ground beside her. My hands hovered near her head.

"Mother?" My voice broke. My body trembled.

Joseph didn't speak. His eyes couldn't meet mine. But they were full of tears.

I buried my face next to hers—my real mother.

"Someone help her! Please! She has to live!"

Before the moment could break again—five soldiers rushed in, lifted her carefully, and jogged toward the unknown.

I sat in the dust, blood on my hands.

Hugging myself.

Crying harder.

Harder.

Joseph knelt beside me and gently placed his arm over my shoulder.

Eyes shut tight.

And nothing else. Only the stars.

Only the fire.

Mother...

Chapter XXVI

"A hospital alone shows what war is"-Erich Maria Remarque

I woke up in another room. It was dark. A clock glowed faintly beside the bed. **03:00 A.M.** The devil's hour—so they say. I never thought much of it. Just childish nonsense. Superstition.

I swung my legs off the bed.

A silver wrapper caught my eye. I reached for it, brought it to my nose. **Food.** I tucked it in my pocket, now wide awake, drawn to the door.

I had to see her. Lia. Locked doors couldn't stop me.

A gentle beeping echoed from one of the rooms. I crept toward the sound, barely breathing. I opened the door without a sound.

There she was.

A pulse oximeter blinked beside her long, sterile bed. Tubes of color—bright, strange liquids—connected to her. My mother. She wasn't dead. Somehow.

I stood beside her. No tears left. Only numbness.

I sat in a chair nearby and closed my eyes.

I was ten.

Everyone was watching TV. Dixie with her dolls, Ford chatting with stepmother, stepfather glued to the screen.

I watched from the stairs—then quietly retreated to my basement bedroom. My Lego set lay scattered. Ford had thrown it once, called it "too dusty." But I'd rebuilt it. My hands moved the tiny figures while I munched an apple I'd stolen from the kitchen.

It was peaceful. No questions. Just silence.

Morning arrived.

The room was brighter, but my soul wasn't.

I looked at mother—her eyes were shut. Those green eyes… gone.

I stared at nothing. A ghost blink. No movement. No sound.

Then, footsteps. I didn't look up, but I saw her in the corner of my eye. A little girl. Maybe six.

Finally, I turned my head. My hands pressed together at my chin. I didn't speak.

"Hello," said the girl.

She was chubby-faced, wearing a sage-green dress and clutching a stuffed bear. Her eyes—deep brown. Her red hair glinted in the sun—like Stella's.

Still, I didn't respond.

"Do you know where Mama is?" Her voice squeaked, soft and trembling.

I shook my head.

"What's your name?"

"Alice." I spoke quietly. "Where are your parents?"

"Papa left us. Mama was taken. Someone said they found her with my baby brother."

I sat up straighter.

"I live in the orphanage across the street," she said, pointing out the window behind me. A brick building with long windows. Words I couldn't read carved across the front.

The mother... she had to be somewhere here.

"Come."

I stood, took the girl's hand. My eyes stung from exhaustion. My feet moved door to door.

Some rooms were empty. Others whispered life through machines.

Then—we found her.

Still cradling her baby, she sat quietly beneath a blanket. She looked up as we entered.

"Madeline?" Her voice, raspy but gentle.

"Mama!" The little girl ran to her mother's side. Jealousy gripped me. My mind. My heart. My stomach.

The mother looked at me. Softly. "Thank you, love."

I nodded once. And walked away.

Chapter XXVII

"The woods are lovely, dark and deep. But I have promises to keep, and miles to go before I sleep"-Robert Frost

I was sick of this place. I was sick of myself. I was sick of the guns. I was sick of the uniforms. I was sick of the tight buns and the stupid poker face. I was sick of the pain, of the masked figures. I was fucking sick of war.

I strapped my gun to my back. And searched for an exit.

But I stopped— Where had Connor gone?

My arm ached again. Someone had looped a strap over my neck, supporting it. Not swollen. Just useless.

Wide stairs. Small steps. One nearly took me out. A door to the left with a square window offered hope. Escape.

I trudged toward it.

Warm air spilled through the crack—like a long-lost friend. I'd missed this. But the view?

Horror.

The base was demolished, burned from afar.

A silhouette stood off in the distance. *Naomi?*

I walked, careful. Closer. It was her.

She had a scar now—dragged across her cheek, near her eye. A tattoo on her arm. *Till we meet again.*

"Alice!" she cried, pulling me into a suffocating hug. Naomi was taller now. Stronger.

"Where is everyone? What happened? Is Connor still out there?" My voice cracked. Breath short. Panic creeping back.

"I haven't heard from them."

"I want to go back. Please! I can't lose anyone else!" I gasped, trembling.

"Alice, calm down. We'll find them. But your arm—"

"No! I don't care. I'm leaving!" I stormed toward the nearest tank.

Naomi didn't try to stop me. Instead, she jumped inside.

"Well? You coming in?"

I climbed in.

We drove. Fast. Others joined—tanks charging toward Valkros. The heat suffocated us as we returned to the beginning.

That building—the one where the woman and her child were found.

But the soldiers waiting weren't ours.

Naomi arched ahead. Fast.

The masked troops turned and opened fire.

Smoke swallowed us whole.

I ducked behind a mound of sand. Each shot was returned. Fire. Hide. Fire. Hide.

Once. Twice. Until silence.

I ran low to the ground, toward the building. The door was gone—only shattered bricks.

Please... Connor... anyone...

No tears left. Just air and prayer.

Inside, nothing.

It didn't feel right.

A cough.

Small. Fragile. Childlike.

I turned toward the sound. Eyes drooping. Head spinning. A stench hit me. Toxic. Not the air I remembered.

Groaning followed the cough. I marched forward, step by step.

A shadow. Curled. Human. I leaned in. Adjusting to the dark. A boy. Tan-skinned. Maybe four.

"Are... Are you going to hurt me?" he whispered.

"No. Do you trust me?"

He looked up. Shook his head. Backed into the corner.

"You're safe with me. I promise."

He tried to stand, fell hard. So thin. I scooped him up—weightless.

"I want food," he said.

My pocket pressed against my leg.

The granola bar. Silver-wrapped.

I opened it with my teeth and gave it to him.

He took one bite. Another. Then grabbed it, clinging tight.

I ran with him in my arms.

BEEP. Silence shattered.

BEEP. Faster.

A bomb? No one was left. That couldn't be it.

Beep. Beep. Beep. The speed doubled. Tripled.

I bolted.

The sun hit my face just as I got outside.

Then—

Eruption.

Smoke. Fire. Shrapnel flying. Wind knocked me back.

The boy cried in my arms.

I didn't stop. I ran. Through desert wind and ash.

Chapter XXVIII

"Finding someone who's willing to drown with you creates a situation where you no longer want to drown"-Marilyn Manson

We were celebrating in the cafeteria.

In just a few days, we had saved three prisoners. It had become our home—our sleeping quarters, our refuge. Everything else was gone. The little boy was hugged and kissed by soldiers, cheered like a victory. They tried to get the Woman to celebrate too, but she just sat motionless on her mattress. Her baby was dead.

The little girl twirled her stuffed teddy bear for everyone, beaming. She didn't know the truth. Not yet.

I looked at the Woman again—Joseph sat beside her, offering water. Still no sign of Connor.

It didn't make sense. Henry was back. Stella and Ruby too.

Had they forgotten him? The quiet boy with the photographic memory? I stopped cheering. My heart wasn't in it anymore.

This wasn't fair.

I left the cafeteria, cradling my injured arm, biting back anger. Footsteps followed behind me.

"Hot out here, ain't it?" Henry stood with his hands on his hips, gazing up at the sky.

"Where is Connor?" I demanded.

He blinked. "Isn't he with you?"

"No, Henry. Please don't tell me you lost him!" The panic cracked through my voice. "We were just attacked. He could be dead."

Henry froze. His face twisted. *What have I done?* Read loud in his eyes.

"We have to go," I said quietly.

He didn't argue. He led me to a new tank—smaller, darker. Deep green. The seats were strangely comfortable.

We hadn't even adjusted when he slammed the pedal. The wheels screamed against dirt.

"Stop driving so fast!" I shouted.

He didn't listen. His jaw clenched tight. This wasn't the Henry I knew. I missed the goofy one.

We arrived.

Not the tall building from before—this one was wide, squat, ugly.

"Where are we?" I asked, gripping my gun.

Connor didn't have one. He couldn't defend himself.

"If they took him," Henry said, "he has to be here."

No guards.

No barriers.

That wasn't right.

Henry paused near a low hole. A gun poked out from the shadows. He sidestepped and fired.

Three bursts. I dropped my weapon and covered my ears, drowning in the sound.

"Henry, where is he?" I asked, desperate.

"In here."

"What if they're armed?"

"They're not."

"How do you know?"

"Because I was taken!"

I stared at him.

"What?" But he moved ahead, kicking the door. It didn't budge. Another kick. It slammed open.

Empty.

Henry rushed down the hall. The room ahead was missing a door—just a wide opening with three chairs and one table. Figures in shadow. Guns raised. Eyes sharp.

Henry spoke in another language. I felt ignorant. I didn't know a word.

Ten guns pointed toward us.

I lifted mine. Not to shoot—just to survive. They couldn't see my heart. Couldn't see how it burned for a boy left behind.

A masked man locked eyes with me. He raised his gun.

"Why are you here?"

"Where is he?" My voice held steady. I was proud of that.

Another man dragged Connor into view—gripping his shirt like an object. He threw him to the ground. Kicked him.

"What are you doing?" I cried. "STOP!"

Henry pulled my arm back, as ten weapons pointed at me.

I broke free.

"Don't you *dare* kill him!"

The masked man sneered. "We've been looking for someone special like him. He's ours. Leave now—or die." He prodded my shoulder with his gun.

"No! Take me instead! He's slow—leave him!"

"Alice!" Henry whispered, gesturing to retreat.

"You can't leave him!" I cried. "You've gone mad!"

They kept kicking.

Connor made no sound. He was holding a piece of paper. The same paper chief held when he was called a genius.

"Take me!" I shouted. "I'll do anything you ask. Mark my words!"

The masked man paused, thinking. I couldn't see his face—just eyes calculating.

"Trust me. He's slow!" I hated myself as I said it. But I'd trade my life to stop their boots. "I'll be your hostage. Your soldier. Just let him go!"

They didn't stop. Connor covered his mouth, choking down screams.

Henry dragged me away.

"NO! PLEASE!"

We reached the tank. He shoved me inside.

"You didn't even try!" I wept. "He's just a boy! He's autistic! You're unbelievable!"

"They would've killed us," Henry said, staring into the road.

"I'd rather die than see that again."

"You don't know anything."

"I know you don't abandon an autistic soldier to be tortured!"

"You know why they took me, Alice? I fought for her."

"For who?"

"My mother!"

Silence. Then rage.

"Why didn't we fight? There were two of us!"

"I don't know! I love Connor—I truly do. But he's probably dead."

"Don't say that!"

"Alice, the world isn't all cupcakes and rainbows."

"How dare you! You have no idea what I've seen. I'm no ostrich burying its head in the sand."

The rest of the ride was shouting. Arguing. And then—quiet. Quiet that stung.

I chose a mattress at the far corner of the cafeteria. No one slept there. It was cold. Right by the roar of the air conditioning. That hum was my lullaby now. Maybe if I got sick, they'd let me leave. I curled into myself—cast pressed to my stomach.

Everyone else was asleep. The air shut off. A tear rolled down my nose. Finally, I thought. Another followed. And another. And another.

Connor.

Has anyone ever asked how much a boy is worth?

Tonight, to me— Connor was worth everything.

Chapter XXIX

"There is a sacredness in tears. They are not the mark of weakness, but of power. They speak more eloquently than ten thousand tongues. They are the messengers of overwhelming grief, of deep contrition, and of unspeakable love"-Washington Irving

We were off again. My group had left without me. *Had they forgotten me too?* Maybe. I didn't mind.

I returned to the mysterious room where I'd woken up days before. Where Mother had been found. I peeked through the crease of the door. The hum of machines was gone. Her life support—shut off.

"No. No, no, no, no, no!"

A woman stood at the end of the hallway.

"Did you cut her life support?" I asked.

She looked guilty.

"Miss, we didn't think she would live—"

"And? That's out of the question! Her heart was beating, wasn't it?" She flinched at my voice—then fled into another room.

I screamed. And screamed. And screamed. Louder and louder and louder.

Doors locked. People watched me fall apart and did nothing.

"He killed her!" I shouted staring at the people trying to hide. "He killed her! He killed her!"

Two men grasped my arms trying to calm me down. But I let go. Pushing them far from my trauma. They attempted again.

"Let me go! You sick people!"

I ran back into the room. Mother's room. I reattached every wire, every tube—hands shaking. I pounded the pulse oximeter.

"I just wanted to say goodbye!"

I shook her, over and over. I checked her pulse. Wrist. Neck. Heart. It was no use.

I buried my face into her arm, as the men stood at the doorway.

"Leave! Leave and never touch me again! I'm broken can't you see? You blind pieces of crap!" I turned back to the corpse. "Mother, please… Just one minute. That's all it takes."

I was being carried through an airport. I remember very little.

Mother was beside me—crying. A man held me. Brown hair, dark eyes, tan skin. His eyes—red. Had he just finished crying? Was that man my father?

A mirror stood near her bed.

They want you to cry, I thought. *But you... You will never cry again.* My father must be alive, but now— I felt senseless. No more tears. My eyes grew dark.

I saw a knife resting on the coffee table. I picked it up. I stood before the mirror. And made three light cuts on my left cheek.

Pain... will teach pain.

Blood trickled down. I gathered my hair. Braided it. Twice. No tight bun today.

I looked at her one last time. And walked away.

Till we meet again

Chapter XXX

"Somewhere deep down there's a decent man in me, he just can't be found"-Eminem

I made it my mission to sacrifice everything for Connor. If selling myself was the answer—so be it.

Joseph was laughing in the cafeteria, surrounded by others. I grabbed his ear from behind and yanked him outside.

"Ow! Alice, let go!" So I did—with a rip. He fell to the ground. "What are you doing?" he hissed, clutching his ear.

"You're horrible, Joseph! Do you even know where your brother is?"

He stared at me, rattled. "He's not with you?"

"Enough! Why is it always my job to protect *your* family?" I leaned closer, my voice like steel. "I know where he is. And you'd better pray he's alive."

"Where?" He began to cry. I'd never seen him cry.

But I wouldn't cry for him. Not now.

"We're bringing everyone. You convince Henry to find him. Beg, cry—I don't care. We're leaving."

He nodded quickly and hobbled away toward the cafeteria, still clutching his torn ear. I stared at the Polaroid in my hand.

Mother... if you're listening. I will win. I will. For you.

Sudden motion jolted me. Pushing. Running. I slipped the photo into my pocket.

"You're welcome," Joseph said, adjusting the bandage on his ear. No more tears. He'd gathered fifty soldiers. Some stayed back for safety.

I scanned the crowd. No Henry. Hundreds of tanks fired up, all moving in one direction.

"Where's Henry?" I asked Joseph.

"He says he's not feeling well."

Pathetic.

"What happened to your face?" he asked, eyeing the three scars.

"Don't worry about it."

We arrived at the same wide building. Still no guards. Soldiers stormed the entrance. I ran inside.

A masked man stood in the shadows, his eyes locked on mine. His mouth was hidden—but the grin stretched into his eyes.

I turned and ran outside. Vomited. Wiped my mouth with my sleeve. Then ran back in.

Those who once frightened me will learn regret.

Gunshots echoed. I didn't flinch. I ran deeper inside.

At the end of the hallway, the masked man gripped Connor by the shoulder.

"Leave him," I said, raising my gun.

He fired.

Missed.

Was it luck? Faith? Me?

"Let me just speak," I said, raising one hand.

He didn't care.

More gunshots. Not at me. *Around* me. Mocking me. He laughed with each shot. Connor was coughing blood.

"What have you done to him!"

No answer. Just more laughter. More bullets. Each shot crept closer. My arm trembled from holding the gun.

"If you kill him, what was this all for?" I tried to reason with him. "You'd lose the brilliance of the boy you wanted!"

The shooting stopped. So did the laughter.

Then— From the shadows behind him...

A single shot.

Straight to the head.

Chapter XXXI

"I feel safe in white because deep down inside, I'm an angel"- Sean Combs

He was masked too. Why would he kill his own? His friend. His troop. His soldier.

Connor dropped to the ground, blood bubbling from his mouth. If I went to him—he'd kill me. If I stayed put—he'd kill Connor.

"Show mercy," I said. "He's just a boy."

No answer. Not one word. He gripped Connor's neck and slammed him to the ground. Again. Again. Again.

I shot him. All the strength I had left pulsed through one last bullet. It knocked him out.

I crawled toward Connor. "Can you hear me?" My walkie-talkie crackled against my chest. "I have Connor!" I shouted.

I lifted him over my shoulders. That round, chubby face—now hollowed and sharp. His jawline carved deep. Strong.

"I'm coming to the front. Wait there."

I pushed through bodies. Soldiers parted. Everyone stared.

Connor's mouth was caked in dried blood. His eyes—shut.

I checked his pulse. Alive.

I handed him off to Adam. Same age as Henry. Twenty-two. Adam always stood by Henry. Loyal. But Henry? His lies still burn through me. Sure, he lost people. Everyone pities him. Nobody ever pitied me.

Scrubbing dishes was all I got. Joseph stood in the back. I saw those eyes. Bright blue. Impossible to miss.

He mouthed: *Thank you.* I gave a single nod. Just one. My gesture.

Gunfire echoed from outside. The guards had been hiding in deep pits—clever. Some would call it tactical genius. I called it cowardice.

War is an unfair game.

That's why they took Connor. I lied once—said he was slow. He wasn't. He's brilliant. Remembers everything—even from the womb. That's the danger.

Chief wasn't smart bringing him here. No gun. Just a brain.

Every time I blinked, he was there. The masked man. Even in silence. Even in stillness.

What had gotten into me? Trauma?

No. Not fear. Not anymore.

I made a promise:

I will never put fear on myself. Always, and forever.

Chapter XXXII

"I like creating beauty out of scary things"-Grimes

I was cleaning the dried blood from my arms in the sink. Some were awake. Some had gone to check on Connor. I washed my face. The cuts stung. I didn't flinch. I didn't speak.

Henry sat in the far corner of the cafeteria, staring at the floor. *Traitor.* I would never forget the moment he left Connor behind. Connor being alive was a miracle. A gift.

I closed my eyes, trying to summon another memory— But all I saw was the masked man.

The masked man.

It didn't make sense. Why had his own partner shot him?

I tossed and turned on my mattress, searching for comfort. I shifted to my left and saw the Woman, still holding her dead child. She cradled him near her chin, mumbling words I couldn't hear.

Tomorrow was my birthday. I wasn't excited.

I'd learned to forget it. But part of me still wanted to remember.

So I did. I closed my eyes.

The masked man.

I shot them open again.

I couldn't keep living like this. Why? Why? Why?

I sat up, hands gripping my scalp. My breathing grew deliberate. Eyes darting everywhere. And again— Every time I blinked, I saw him.

He wasn't dead. I felt it. I knew it.

Stella was talking to Ruby in the middle of the cafeteria. I walked over.

"Can I sit with you guys? I can't sleep."

Stella looked at me, confused. "Yeah, sure."

They continued talking. Drip. Drip. The sound of blood. The blood I remembered pouring from my arm.

I listened quietly.

Apparently, Ruby liked Henry.

I was told to keep it to myself.

"Why Henry?" I asked. "Out of everyone—why him?"

"We've been friends since childhood," Ruby said.

I looked down at my feet. The masked man's eyes— A dark look of death.

I clasped my hands together and returned to my mattress. I stared at my boots.

I have to go back.

Chief barged into the quiet cafeteria. Nurses followed, wheeling in long beds. Twenty bodies. Bloody.

Chief stopped at Henry's corner.

"Bandages?" he asked.

Henry handed him five rolls. The nurses got to work.

Each body was nearly mummified in gauze. Arms, necks, stomachs, faces—covered in blood. *What had happened to them?*

Chief left the nurses and stepped into the center of the room.

"Of course they've killed more," he said. "We even lost some on the way to Valkros. Tomorrow will be a new day. I'll be taking new soldiers for our next journey. Everyone must keep training. It's for our country's sake."

With those bold words, he exited. Some looked confused. Others whispered quickly. *What if there is no tomorrow?* What if they kill us all? Nuke us?

I used my fingernail to draw on the hard cement floor.

A sketch of Mother.

I wished I had green paint—for her eyes. A fine pencil—for each strand of her hair. White—for her bright smile. Skin tone—for her dimples. Just like mine.

The sketch was perfect. I pressed my index and middle fingers together, kissed them, and gently placed them on her image.

Oh, the misery.

I had succeeded in my one dream— To meet family. Even if just for a minute. I had days with Lia. That's what I chose to remember. Not her death. I lay down. Closed my eyes.

Hello, masked man. Till we meet again.

Chapter XXXIII

"It is lovely, when I forget all birthdays, including my own, to find that somebody remembers me"-Ellen Glasgow

I sat on the sand. Some people were practicing their shooting. Others were talking, doing sit-ups. Our team was preparing new rockets. I didn't feel like training. Not today. It was my birthday, after all.

It felt like hours. My thighs were burning. I was probably sunburnt. But I had company.

Joseph, Naomi, Ruby, and Stella came over, forming a circle around me. Not just friends. Family. Then, without a word, they all stood up and walked away— Each in a different direction.

Weird.

Moments later, they returned. Each holding a black box.

"Happy birthday, Alice!" they said in unison.

I didn't like the attention. I'd never received a birthday gift before.

"How did you guys know the date?" I asked, trying to sound meek.

My heart was racing— A million beats per second. *What had they gotten me?*

"Chief mentioned it to us a couple of days ago, when you were away," Naomi said, handing me her box.

"Thank you."

I opened it.

Inside— A beautiful gold bracelet, small pearls wrapped around it in an elegant touch.

"Oh my, Naomi, it's lovely. Thank you!" I hugged her as she helped me fasten it around my wrist.

Joseph handed me his box next. I opened it.

A brand-new pair of earrings. Just for me.

I looked up, shocked.

"I can't take this," I said, placing the lid back on the box and handing it to him.

"No, you keep it. Auntie helped me with the money, don't worry," he said, beaming. Real diamonds nestled in the crevasse of the gold. They glimmered in the sunlight.

"So?" he asked.

"I love it. Thank you!" I hugged him, placing the earrings gently back in the box.

Again and again— Box after box. Hug after hug. Thank you after thank you.

I had the biggest smile I'd ever worn. Suddenly, I had energy. To train. To move. To fight. Pull-ups. Shooting. Swimming. Running. Carrying. Anything you ask— I'll do it.

I slid on the new shoes Ruby bought me. It felt like walking on a soft cloud. Just like the ones Ms. Berg had given me.

Except this time— They were blue, with hints of orange, black, and white.

My first birthday. A dream birthday.

I took a breath after all the exercise. Looked at the dark boxes scattered around me. Their glossy surfaces reflected the sun.

No.

The masked man.

Even now— He came to ruin my mood?

Chapter XXXIV

"Good people do not need laws to tell them to act responsibly, while bad people will find a way around the laws"-Plato

It was Saturday, which meant I got to spend the weekend at Ms. Berg's mansion. I stayed in the same vivid, modern room. She even filled the drawers with new clothes. *Was this paradise?*

I left my room feeling amazing. All the dried, crusty blood was finally off me.

"Well, good morning, Alice," Ms. Berg said, laying down a plate stacked with pancakes and berries.

"Good morning, Ms. Berg."

I was in a good mood. I sat on the high chair, already digging in.

The army had stripped my body of its chubby baby fat. Now I had a well-earned six-pack I wanted to keep— But I couldn't expect not to bloat after a sweet breakfast like this.

Later, I met up with Joseph at the park near Ms. Berg's house. The park was full of rich-looking kids. Tennis and basketball courts. A massive soccer field attached to a playground.

A dream of its own.

I dragged myself behind Joseph, unfamiliar with everything and everyone.

We joined a group of boys and girls around our age. Some girls wore matching tennis skirts, rackets, and tops. Some boys wore soccer or basketball jerseys.

Joseph chatted with the boys while I studied each face, memorizing them.

"Hey Joe, who's the funny-looking girl next to you?" one of the boys asked.

He was pale, with black hair and the darkest eyes I'd ever seen. His accent wasn't Herdonian. It was charming.

"Asher, this is Alice. Alice, Asher," Joseph introduced.

"You're not from here, are you, Alice?"

A pretty girl next to Asher swung her tennis racket, eyeing me from head to toe.

"Well, no. I recently moved—"

"That's nice. Why don't you sit over there on that bench while we play?" she cut me off. Joseph didn't look amused.

"Can't she play with us?" he asked.

"Does she have a racket? No? Then I guess you know the answer," she said, laughing with two other girls behind her. She placed her hand on Joseph's shoulder, encouraging him to laugh along. Except the loyal man swayed her hand away standing beside me.

"I don't like tennis anyway," I said, glaring at her.

"I've never met someone with such poor taste in sports."

She stood in front of me. Tall—like Naomi.

Try me, I wanted to say.

"Hannah, don't try to intimidate. It's not working," Joseph said.

Hannah. I didn't like her.

She had straight blonde hair, hazel eyes, and freckles that faded across her cheeks. Her ponytail was tied back with a white tennis cap that matched her skirt.

Ms. Berg had great taste in fashion. I wore the new shoes Ruby gifted me, Naomi's bracelet, black shorts, and a bright white shirt from Ms. Berg. It fit tight—something I wasn't used to— But it complemented how thin and muscular I'd become.

The three girls walked to the tennis court.

"Alice, do you play soccer?" Asher asked.

"No. I don't really trust myself with sports."

"Bummer. We're missing one player." I turned to Joseph. *Did he play soccer?*

"What?" he said, staring back.

"Do you play soccer?"

"Well yeah, but what are you going to do if I play?"

"Read. Watch. I don't know." I lazily lifted my arms in the air.

"Do you guys have an extra jersey?"

I sat on a bench near a tree. A book rack stood beside me. I grabbed a book titled *A Dream Land*.

Suddenly, a tennis ball flew toward me, hitting the bench just inches away.

"Watch it!" I yelled.

Hannah ran over to grab the ball.

"Sorry, didn't see you there," she laughed. An ugly, filthy laugh.

I stared back at my book. The cover was blue with white stars. A graveyard. A ghost holding a man's hand. The ghost was a girl in a white dress.

I opened the first page. Reading was hard, but I tried.

Another neon green ball hit the bench.

Hannah and her friends laughed as they ran to retrieve it— But I grabbed it first.

"Give me the ball," she said, pressing forward.

"I'll think about it," I replied, tossing the ball lightly in the air.

I stared into her eyes. Stared until I saw my reflection.

"I don't think you know how to play tennis very well if you keep aiming toward me." I smiled.

"Give it."

She shoved me, making me fall back onto the bench.

I stood up.

Yes, she was tall— But she didn't look like she could carry a brick. She was more model than muscle. Her friends said nothing. Didn't defend her.

Those who aren't real don't deserve to be in your life. I learned that the hard way.

"So here's how I work, Hannah." I pushed the ball hard against her chest. "I don't like when people are rude to me. "So either you fix your attitude— Or leave." I grinned.

She grimaced, grabbing the ball with both hands. Her long, fake nails got in the way. She dropped it.

"You don't look like the type of person to be in this park. You leave."

She shoved me again— Her hands landing directly on my cast.

I flinched at the pain. *You have no idea where that cast came from, Hannah.*

But I got up.

I remembered the three scars I drew on my face.

Each one a rule:**No fear. No tears. No pain.**

I grabbed her shirt— And punched her in the nose.

Blood dripped from her nostrils.

I walked away.

Chapter XXXV

"I like seeing good people win"-Mac Miller

A week had gone by, however life feels still. Connor filled a dark hole in my heart, Joseph isn't the jolly man I met on the train, and mother. . . Well, mother never changed in my soul.

I asked if I could borrow a bike from Ms. Berg's garage. Embarrassing as it was, I couldn't ride a bike. Nobody ever taught me. I hopped on and immediately fell off, catching myself with my right foot.

I kept trying. Again. Again. And again.

Eventually, my balance held. I breathed deeply— In through my nose, out through my mouth. Again. Again. *What if I fell? What if I hurt my arm?*

I gripped the handlebars tightly and looked ahead. My legs pedaled slowly, wobbling to keep balance. Then faster. Faster. The wind blew in my face. It felt nice. Refreshing.

The hospital parking lot was full. People chatted near trees. Others headed to their cars. I rode toward the bike rack. Only three bikes were locked there—one bright green, two black like mine.

I headed toward the building. It reminded me of the old one.

Mother...

Inside, a nurse sat at reception. Two people waited in line. An old man at the front was yelling.

"You think I'll pay this? It's ridiculous! Bills like this for a two-day visit? Bah! Can I get a discount?"

I reached into my pocket, grasping the Polaroid. Let go. Held some quarters I'd found at the park.

"Sir, we can't control our costs," the nurse said. "The only thing I can help you with is checking your insurance—"

"Bah! I ain't got no time for insurance! Just swipe the card already!"

The nurse looked nervous as she took his card and swiped it. I'd never seen a card machine in person before. How interesting. The man stormed out, shoving me slightly as he passed.

I turned toward one of the doors, ready to daydream. I opened my eyes wide.

He was there. The masked man.

Only his eyes visible. He was grabbing someone—Joseph.

"Let him go!" I screamed. No use.

The masked man killed him. I thought he'd been shot. I thought he was gone. Over. Dead.

"Miss?" The receptionist broke my trance. I blinked, staring blankly at her. "Can I help you?" she asked, concerned.

"Yes, I'm sorry. I'm here to visit Connor Witz."

"Ah, yes. He's in room 206," she said.

"Thank you." I read her name tag. Sharon.

She smiled. I walked away.

An elevator waited at the end of the hall. Next to it, a bell hung from the wall. A patient in a wheelchair approached the bell. She rang it. Once. Twice. Three times. Doctors clapped. Cheered. She had no hair. No eyebrows. No eyelashes.

Just skin.

But she smiled.

"Congratulations, Addie!" one of the doctors said.

I'd never seen someone so sick. So bare. So radiant. She looked into my eyes and smiled.

Her wheelchair rolled closer.

"Hello," she said.

"Hi," I replied, matching her soft tone.

"I like your hair," she said, admiring my thick, dark brown waves.

"Thank you."

"I can't wait for mine to grow back. I hope it's as pretty as yours."

"Hope it doesn't have as many knots as mine!" I joked.

She laughed.

"You're wearing an army badge," she said, pointing to the pin on my black shirt.

"I am."

"You're in the army?"

I nodded.

"Why are you in the hospital?"

I looked away, searching for words. "My friend got injured. I must see him." I choked on the last word.

"I'm sorry," she said gently. "I hope he feels better soon." She smiled again. "I'm Addie, by the way."

"Alice."

With that last word, I stepped into the elevator.

Chapter XXXVI

"I have made this letter longer than usual, only because I have not had the time to make it shorter"-Blaise Pascal

Connor lay in his hospital bed. Still. In a coma. His small face was covered in purple bruises and bloody scratch marks.

I felt like an idiot. I had made a promise. Just one promise. I took the sticky notes from his side table. Light yellow. I wrote:

I'm sorry, Connor. It's all my fault. I should have saved you sooner.

—Alice

Day after day, I wrote. Each note placed on the wall. Bus ride after bus ride, just to leave another apology. The wall was yellow now. Not painted. Covered in regret.

Connor never woke up.

Joseph sat beside him today. Holding his hand. Eyes closed. He had been writing notes too. His were green.

"I'll never forgive myself, you know," I said. My voice cracked the silence.

Joseph nodded, still holding Connor's hand. I reached into my pocket. Found the Polaroid. Its sharp edge met my fingers. I didn't flinch.

Pain would have to learn to pain itself.

My arm had healed. The only scars left were the pink gummies I took for my back, and the three red claw marks on my cheek.

I lay on my mattress. Everyone else asleep. he cafeteria was cold today. Just like my heart. I hugged my pillow. Closed my eyes.

The masked man.

I opened them. Closed again.

The masked man.

Harder this time.

The masked man.

I ripped strands of my hair. Again. Again.

Open. *Masked man.* Open again. *Masked man.*

I rolled on my mattress. Roughly. Closed my eyes.

Masked man.

I forced my eyes open. Wide.

I got off the mattress. Grabbed my gun. My smoke mask. Barefoot on cold concrete. Still in pajamas— Black tank top with loose straps. Navy blue sweatpants.

A shadow in the distance.

There he is.

My arms trembled as I raised the gun.

"How did you find me? Who are you?" I called into the dark.

"I am not who you think I am," he said. "But I'm not afraid to shoot you."

"Neither am I." Confidence surged through me. He flinched.

"You will work for me," he said.

"Never."

The cafeteria door creaked open. A figure stood in the doorway. Dark. Unclear.

I looked ahead.

He was gone.

"Alice? What are you doing out here? It's dangerous!" Ruby's voice hissed.

"I—I thought I heard a noise. But it was nothing."

I walked toward her. But I felt it. A pair of eyes. Watching me from behind. Smiling.

I will never sell myself to a monster who hurts the people I love.

N E V E R...

Chapter XXXVII

"The best revenge is to live on and prove yourself"-Eddie Vedder

Dear future me,

Is this war over? Is Connor alive? Are you happy? Do you have a family?

Sincerely, Alice Tillen

My pen ran out of ink.

I folded the letter and tucked it into my backpack.

Outside, the camp was quiet. Everyone had left for Valkros. I'd excused myself with a lie— "I feel like throwing up."

Truth was, I was scared. Valkros was dangerous. Many had died there. My soul was one of them. Joseph didn't go either. He hadn't been the same since his brother. Still, we took the bus to Ms. Berg's for the day.

At the park, Joseph went off to play soccer. I sat on my usual bench.

Someone flicked my ear from behind. Hannah.

"Ow," I said, covering my ear.

"Alice, I think we got off on the wrong foot," she said. "I was thinking you could play tennis with us. I have an extra racket."

"No thanks," I replied coldly.

"Come on! It'll be fun!" She grabbed my arm, tugging me toward the tennis court.

"I really don't know how to play," I said, trying to keep up.

She shoved the racket into my hands and walked backward to her side of the court. Her friends watched from the metal benches. I stood there, hiding behind the racket, gripping it with both hands.

She hit the ball. It came straight at me.

I dodged it.

Her friends laughed. So did Hannah.

"Hannah, I'm really not into tennis," I said.

I placed the racket on the colored concrete floor. It had a bouncy texture.

"Oh, but wait! You must be thirsty!" She ran off with two of her friends to a nearby table.

I wasn't thirsty. They came back holding a huge bowl of water.

"Did you guys run out of cups?" I asked, eyeing the icy bowl.

"Nope!" she said, and dumped it over my head.

I slipped. Fell on my back.

The pain returned. Sharp. Familiar.

Everyone laughed. I had no words.

"Whoops! I'm so sorry!" she said.

I stood up, soaked. Not from sweat— From freezing water. I kept myself from strangling her.

"I was hot anyway," I said calmly. She stopped laughing. "Thanks, Hannah. I think you're making an effort to be my friend." I grinned. Walked away.

I hope to come across you again.

Chapter XXXVIII

"My best friend is the one who brings out the best in me"-
Henry Ford

Happy birthday, Connor—already nineteen! I left you a tiny gift. I hope you enjoy it.

—Alice

Trying to sound optimistic was hard. I didn't write my last name. I couldn't find the guts today. The deep lump in my throat kept me from laughing and celebrating his birthday as he lay there—half dead, half alive. Like a fortune cookie could tell if he would live. Though maybe all it would say is: *"It all depends on you."*

Joseph hasn't talked to me in a very long time. It feels like an eternity. I don't blame him. Every night, I tell myself again and again that it's my fault Connor is in a coma.

Have you ever wondered how strong a friendship can be? Mine ended because of an accident. Just one accident.

I didn't drink water today. The hospital's water fountain was the best thing that ever happened to me. The cold, refreshing water slipped down my throat, making me feel alive again.

With each sip, drops splashed onto my scars—making them burn.

I dragged my heavy black boots outside, not looking at the sun this time. I stared at the sand, which had very few curves, making it look like waves.

What's it like to go to the beach? I'd like to know.

I imagined the sand as giant waves people would surf on. The crashing sound put me at ease. Kids building sandcastles. Adults relaxing in beach chairs. Shells being carried away by the current. Salty ocean water that would burn my eyes. *How does it feel?* I asked myself.

A road appeared ahead—long and clean, with bits of sand covering the faded yellow line. I took a deep breath. My walkie-talkie buzzed in my pocket.

"Hello?"

Chapter XXXIX

"Here we are, trapped in the amber of the moment. There is no why"-Kurt Vonnegut

No one. All I heard was a loud hum—like in a horror movie when the TV screen glitches and turns gray. Whispers now filled the other end of the line.

"Who is this?" I yelled.

More buzzing. Louder. It tingled my ears, forcing me to cover my left ear with one hand.

"You know who I am," the voice said.

Him.

The call ended immediately. I shoved the walkie-talkie back into my pocket and stared at my hands. They were shaking. My eyes darted from side to side. I grabbed hold of myself—hugging tighter and tighter. My breaths were out of control, too fast to keep up.

So I ran.

How did he get a hold of me? How? How? How?

The streets grew busier with every step. I headed toward Ms. Berg's.

I shoved past people as I ran. Some yelled, waving whatever they had in their hands. Others just stared.

Her mansion wasn't hard to spot—big and white. The window frames were deep black, and the windows themselves came in all shapes and sizes, making the house look like a castle. A big castle.

Ms. Berg was outside watering her tulips. I kept running and threw my arms around her, still breathing fast and heavy.

"What's wrong, dear?" she asked.

I didn't answer. I just kept hugging her tightly. She set down her watering pot and embraced me.

Please protect me, I wanted to say. But I couldn't.

I had left—to protect.

Chapter XL

"You have to leave the city of your comfort and go into the wilderness of you intuition. What you'll discover will be wonderful. What you'll discover is yourself"-Alan Alda

She had made me a warm cup of tea in one of her antique cups. The porcelain was adorned with delicate engravings in soft blue and pink, with gold lining the rim. I took a sip, burning my tongue as the tea traveled down.

"I don't know what to do," I finally said.

"You must inform your commander," she replied. "Alice, you can't keep living like this—knowing someone is trying to harm you."

I held the tea with both hands, staring into the golden liquid. A reflection appeared.

Me. Not the masked man this time.

"What if he doesn't believe me?"

"Nonsense," she said firmly. "You are one of his top priorities. Make that count."

She sipped her own golden tea. Her cup was pure white, with white engravings. Her red lipstick stained the rim—darker and darker with each sip.

"Why is he after me?"

"I'm not sure, honey. Does he know you? Has he heard of you?"

"That can't be! My name isn't out in the world. How would he find me?"

She sat silently.

"You can't let that man haunt you, Alice. Listen to me—hundreds of Herdonians are dying this very second. You need to act. It's you. No one else. You were chosen to be here. You saved those prisoners. It's all you."

She tapped her index finger against my chest—again and again.

It's you.

Her words echoed in my mind.

"Well, now what do I do? Everyone's already left for Valkros! I left them there!"

"Chief would never have allowed you to go anyway. Valkros is not on our side. They're against us. Your friends have been in the army before. Learn from them—instead of regretting."

Last night, I had a dream. I saw my father—for only a split second. Then everything went dark. Black.

Nothing else. I was alone. Just a heart, pumping.

THEY ARE COMING. Someone whispered in my dream.

F O R

M E...

Chapter XLI

"To me, every hour of the day and night is an unspeakably perfect miracle"-Walt Whitman

I watched the news on the TV. Images of a woman now filled the screen. A soldier stood beside it, holding the antennas to get a signal.

BREAKING NEWS: VALKROS STRIKES AGAIN

The anchor's voice was urgent, barely masking the panic.

"Early this morning, Valkrosian forces launched a surprise assault on the border town of Elmath. Reports confirm over 200 casualties, including civilians and medical personnel. Herdonian defense units were overwhelmed within minutes."

Grainy footage showed buildings crumbling under missile fire, smoke billowing into the sky, and citizens running through the streets clutching children and supplies.

"The attack appears to be retaliation for last week's intelligence breach, when Herdonian operatives intercepted classified Valkrosian communications. Officials fear this may escalate into a full-scale war."

The screen cut to a shaky video taken by a local resident: Valkrosian drones hovering above, dropping small payloads that exploded on impact. Screams echoed in the background.

"General Philip Haven has declared a state of emergency. All military personnel are ordered to report to their stations immediately."

The broadcast ended with a chilling message:

"Stay inside. Stay alert. Herdonia bleeds tonight."

They killed my mother. They've killed my brothers and sisters of Herdonia.

I took out my notepad.

Dear future me,

Once I die, I want to die with a purpose.

Chapter XLII

"Why does the eye see a thing more clearly in dreams than the imagination when awake?"-Leonardo da Vinci

I was standing in line, waiting for the receptionist. The hospital stretched out in front of me—like a strand of yarn unraveling. Your grandmother would yell at you to tighten it back up, but all you wanted was to follow that string to infinity.

One person after the other.

Then it was my turn.

The receptionist smiled. We'd gotten to know each other from all my visits.

"He's awake."

My jaw dropped. I dashed down the hall, slamming the elevator button again and again.

"Hey girl, watch it! Almost made me tip over! Bah! Kids," grumbled a grumpy old man behind me.

Finally—oh finally—Connor's room.

I opened the door. Boxes lay scattered on the floor, presents surrounding him. He looked up.

"Alice!"

I rushed to him, wrapping him in a strong embrace. Like a little brother. I didn't let go. He began to cry.

"Oh, I thought I was going to die!" His skinny arms loosened from my grip.

"I don't have much time with you, so you have to tell me. What did those people do to you?"

"They're heading here. I don't know when. They forced me to give them all the coordinates. I said no, and they started kicking me... feeding me this liquid. They gave me shots until I said something."

It was worse than I thought. Connor's eyes revealed pain and trauma—just like mine. His deep eye bags were purple and black. Still, he had a perfect smile.

"Alice... you need to go. They're coming soon. You can't let them hurt anyone. Please."

I stood beside his bed.

"Never," I replied.

I wanted to cry. But I made a promise. They won't make me cry.

The people of Valkros will cry for eternity after the mistake they just made.

Chapter XLIII

"Freedom means the opportunity to be what we never thought we would be"-Daniel J. Boorstin

Everyday, our group took the bus to Kundra, a city in Herdonia, and stayed the whole day. This time, we made camp to stay overnight. I packed chips I'd stolen from the hospital vending machine. Henry tagged along—by force. He hadn't been the same since our fight. I didn't talk to him.

But most of all, I was angry at Joseph. Connor had finally woken up. I gave everything. What more did he want from me?

Henry stood up and started walking into the darkness.

"Henry!" Naomi hissed. "Where are you going?"

He looked uncomfortable. Then he returned and started grabbing his gun.

"Did you hear something?" Joseph asked. Henry didn't answer.

"Gosh, Henry, answer us!" I yelled.

Stella placed her hand over my mouth as I continued to scream.

He was now in the darkness. With the darkness. His own shadow from the lantern had left him.

A gunshot.

We all jumped at the sound, scrambling to strap on our guns. Thankfully, Henry returned—unwounded—signaling us to follow.

We hid behind a tall building. Henry pointed to an apartment across the street. People were walking inside. But they didn't look like they lived there.

Shot number one. In the apartment.

Shot number two. They had arrived.

We ran inside with our gas masks on. The men turned to us.

Lord.

The masked man.

I froze.

Adam was beside Henry, shooting again and again. Perfect aim. A smile beneath his mask flickered in his eyes.

Joseph grabbed my arm, pulling me upstairs as Adam and Henry held the line.

More soldiers entered different rooms. I headed into one.

Smoke everywhere. A baby crying.

I fired as many bullets as I could, hiding behind a chair with each bang. Ruby held my hand as she shot three.

The door to another room opened. Ruby rushed to console a crying mother.

I darted toward a little boy clutching a letter, sobbing. He spoke Herdonian.

Ruby joined me, translating.

"He was writing to his friends. He wanted to say goodbye," she said.

I walked over to the baby in the father's arms.

"May I see him, sir?"

The man nodded, handing me the baby. I checked the pulse.

"Ruby, Henry needs to check on the baby. He's the only one certified for medical emergencies."

"Henry won't talk to me," she said. "I'm sick of it."

"Me neither. But we can't take any chances."

I gave the baby to Ruby as she walked out. The mother continued to cry. A huge bookshelf had been knocked down— used to barricade the door.

The little boy sat beside his mother, crying with her.

I dropped my backpack and handed a bag of chips to the boy. He stared at me, slowly reaching out.

"I cannot talk... very well," the father said, stuttering.

"We'll communicate as best we can, sir."

He nodded slowly, trying to understand.

I took out smoke masks for everyone and opened the emergency window. Extended stairs zigzagged left and right.

I helped each of them out into the cold night. Colder than I'd ever felt here. It felt... nice.

Adam waited at the bottom, holding Henry by the arm. Blood soaked through Henry's shirt. His uniform had been cut open, revealing a long, deep scar across his stomach.

"Take them back to our camp," Adam told me.

"And Henry? You're not going to let him swell like this?"

He didn't answer. Just spoke into his walkie-talkie.

What had gotten into everyone? Had I done something wrong?

The family was fast asleep in one of the tents. I took out a flashlight from Joseph's bag and grabbed *A Dream Land*.

Footsteps echoed near me. Vibrations danced in my ears.

They had come back.

Henry lay on towels as Adam inspected his wound.

"Oh!" I gasped at the sight of the cut.

"They had knives," Joseph said. Deadly.

"Finally talking?" I snapped.

He shook his head repeatedly.

"What do you want from me?" I yelled.

"Alice," Stella warned, grabbing my shoulder. A hiss escaped Henry's lips.

"Hold still, man. I'm trying to wrap it up," Adam muttered, nearly done dressing the wound.

See? Imagine that—but a bullet in your arm and back, I wanted to say.

I laid on the cold tent floor. Hands behind my head. Eyes closed.

I was with the masked man. Neither of us armed. Just staring—like we wanted to kill each other. It was night, but his body glowed in the darkness. Slowly, he took off his mask, revealing a beard.

Before he could remove it completely—

My dream was over.

Chapter XLIV

"Never interrupt your enemy when he is making a mistake"-Napoleon Bonaparte

A huge tank of soldiers rolled out again. About thirty. They left me behind. Again.

Chief stayed. He sat with Connor, who had finally been discharged.

His arms were twigs. His once-chubby face now sunken, cheekbones sharp. His legs looked like chair legs. His eyes—dark as a computer keyboard.

I wish Joseph would listen to me. Or talk to me. I just need to see those sky-blue eyes I always loved.

If it weren't for Connor, everyone in that apartment would be dead. He's brilliant. And that makes him dangerous. People want his brain—not for the good of all, but for their own twisted use.

"Joseph, will I ever go back to normal?" Connor asked.

Joseph stared at his bony face. But didn't answer. He got up and left.

What is wrong with him?

"Why isn't he talking to me?" Connor's eyes welled with tears.

"I don't know. If only I did. Ever since your accident, he hasn't been the same."

"Is it my fault?"

Chief left the cafeteria, jogging after Joseph.

"No. It never was. You saved so many people yesterday, Connor. If anyone's to blame, it's not you. Joseph's an idiot to think otherwise."

I handed him a spoonful of soup I'd made in the kitchen.

"Can you answer my question, Alice?"

"Sure," I said. "Your face will be good as new. The human body is smart—just like you. It'll take time. Remember when I hurt my back?" Connor nodded. "Well, it'll be like that. Just hope you don't have to take gummies for a whole year to soothe the pain!" I nudged him lightly, joking.

"Connor... when you were in Valkros, did they ask you anything else?"

"There was a man who kept saying your name. He kicked me until my arms and legs were bleeding."

I froze. How dare he threaten Connor.

"Anything else? Did he say anything else?"

"No," he paused. "Why are they masked?"

"I'm not really sure. Even so, I don't want to know. They probably look like pigs."

"Alice! What if they hear you say that? You could get in trouble!"

"Please. I won't be fooled by them. They can try to intimidate me. I know who they are. And I'm not afraid. Neither should you be."

I straightened my badge on my uniform. Connor sipped his soup slowly, the bowl gradually emptying.

"Make sure not to eat too fast, okay?" I patted his shoulder and walked out of the cafeteria.

Chief was gone. Only Joseph remained—sitting on the hot sand, knees pulled to his chest, arms wrapped around them, chin resting on his kneecaps.

"Why are you mad at me?" My voice was sharp. Toxic to the ear.

"I'm not," he muttered.

"I'm no sloth, Joseph. You haven't been the same since we found Connor. And I've already been ignored by Henry. You're not making things any better!"

I clenched my fists and marched toward him.

"Wasn't trying to be a burden." A horrible remark.

"Well," I paused, "you are."

He lifted his chin and looked up at me. And smiled.

"What?"

"Just getting a sense of nostalgia from the first time I met you. Grumpy."

"I am not grumpy!"

Silence.

I turned to see Joseph's face red, trying to hold in laughter. He snorted and burst out laughing. A vein popped at the corner of his forehead.

I beamed, looking up at the sky, letting out a quick laugh.

Without thinking, I nudged him with my elbow. He nudged back, and before I knew it, we were side by side, shoulder to shoulder.

Then he pulled me into a hug—the kind you give someone when words aren't enough but you're not ready to spill your soul.

"Don't get used to that," I said, smirking.

"Too late," he replied.

The tension between us had cracked, just a little. Enough to breathe.

"Now that you're happy again, can you tell me why you were mad at me?" I asked.

"I wasn't mad at you."

"Liar!"

"You missed my point. I wasn't mad at you—I was just angry. At Henry. At the people who almost killed my brother. I took it out on you and the others. It was foolish."

"It was foolish. But I understand. I wasn't grumpy when I first met you. I was distressed. I didn't live in a happy household. I took my pain and passed it onto someone who made me happy again. I can't forgive myself for that."

He nodded, staring at the sand.

"I don't know if I can continue being in the army," I said.

Joseph turned sharply.

"Why?" His voice cracked—higher than usual.

"I've lost too much. I don't think I can handle it anymore."

Don't cry. DON'T. You promised after her death. Blink a tear and face the consequences.

"You're not alone. We need you. You were chosen for a reason. Don't leave it."

He was right. Chief chose me to stay.

A gust of wind brushed my face.

"It doesn't change the fact that there's a man after me. He could be anywhere, Joseph. I saw him one night. I'm scared."

Goosebumps rose on my arms. The masked man haunted me.

Joseph leaned closer and placed a soft kiss on my cheek. He embraced me again.

I took a chance and closed my eyes.

There he was.

Chapter XLV

"Fear cannot be banished, but it can be calm and without panic; it can be mitigated by reason and evaluation"- Vannevar Bush

It felt like hours. We walked. Many had died along the way.

I gripped my gun tighter, eyes shut for a moment. When I opened them, a shed came into view—metal, not wood. I stared at my feet as I moved toward it, Naomi beside me, scanning the area.

Then I stumbled. My heavy black boot jerked back.

A hand. Sticking out from under the shed.

"Naomi," I said, pointing. Her eyes widened, locking with mine.

I stepped inside.

Bodies. Everywhere. Blood soaked the walls, the floor, even the ceiling. I opened my mouth, but nothing came out.

Each step was a struggle—dodging limbs, stepping over twisted torsos. Hundreds. Maybe more.

"Oh Naomi, what do we do?" I gasped.

"We have to call Adam and Henry. Tell them to bring the tanks." Her voice trembled. She ran.

I stayed.

Hands. Legs. Heads. All misplaced. All wrong.

Who did this?

The shed stretched on, a corridor of death. No living soul inside. Just me. And the dead.

Then—two shadows. Far off.

Adam and Henry, my heart said. My brain whispered: *It's him.*

They began loading bodies into tanks. One by one. I watched.

A little girl lay near my feet. Blood on her chest. Eyes wide open.

Adam rolled up his sleeves, revealing dark skin slick with sweat.

Eventually, the shed was empty. They left. I looked down. Dry blood on my boots.

Joseph walked beside me again.

His steps matched mine, quiet and steady. I told him everything. The blood. The bodies. The little girl. He didn't interrupt. Just listened.

"What if they were one of us?" I asked, voice cracking.

"I hope not," he said. His tone was calm. Not cheerful. Not broken. Just… Joseph.

We kept walking.

He glanced at me. "You okay?"

I shook my head. "Not really."

He didn't say anything. Instead, he wrapped his arm around me holding my shoulder. I looked at him.

"Hey," he said, "you're still here. That counts for something."

I smiled. Just barely.

He reached into his pocket and pulled out a crumpled candy wrapper. Held it out like it was treasure.

"Found this earlier. Thought you might want it."

I took it. It was empty.

"You're the worst," I said.

He grinned. "But I made you smile."

We walked a little slower after that. Not because we were tired. Just because it felt okay to.

I wanted to ask where we were going. Who we were fighting. Who would try to kill us next.

But my mind wandered.

How many prisoners are left? How many have died? How many are being whipped to death right now?

I didn't want to walk anymore. My feet ached. Sweat clung to my face.

You can leave me here to perish.

I forced myself forward, catching up to Ruby.

"Where are we heading?" I asked.

"Remember the woman you saved? She said her husband was taken to another camp."

The woman I saved? Or the one who lost her baby?

Two different things. I didn't want credit for her pain. I just wanted to be a soldier. Nothing more. Nothing less.

I fiddled with the Polaroid in my pocket. *Fly high, mother.* Could I say the same for my father?

His face haunted my thoughts. *Was he dead? Or alive? Who was he? Why did he leave?*

Step after step, I reached a small building. I didn't like it. I turned around. No one.

"Joseph? Naomi?" I called out.

Silence.

Then— A tap on my shoulder. I turned slowly.

"Nice to see you again, Alice."

Him.

Chapter XLVI

"For me, my awakening came when I was kidnapped"-Patty Hearst

My eyes were small, but my eyelids felt heavy—swollen with fear.

"What do you want from me? Where is everyone?" He gripped my arm, hard. A gun pressed against my temple.

"Get away from me!" I tore myself from his grip, raising my own weapon.

"Move, I shoot," he said.

I froze.

His face was masked, as always. But his eyes—dark and sharp—spoke every word he didn't say.

Then he grabbed me again. Dragged me. *Where was he taking me? Where? Where? Where?*

He threw me to the ground.

A large room. Cages. Babies crying. Mothers clutching them, eyes wide with terror.

I gripped my gun tighter. Every time I tried to raise it, something stopped me.

"Why are you after me? How did you find me?" I regretted asking. He said nothing. "I'll do anything! Just show sympathy—I'm only eighteen!"

He pointed the gun again. Fired.

Not at me. Just beside me.

I flinched. *Why didn't he kill me?*

I looked around. Terrified mothers. Daughters. Huddled together in cages.

"I'm not interested in killing you," he said.

But the gun aimed at my forehead said otherwise. His words were weapons. Each syllable cut deeper than the last.

"Then why are you after me?" I tried to hide the tremble in my voice.

"You see all these people, Alice?" He gestured to the cages—young women, children, packed inside like animals.

I nodded. Barely.

"If you don't do as you're told, they'll all be executed." He smiled. Not with his mouth. With his eyes. A twisted, vile smile.

"You're horrible!"

He fired again. This time, the bullet hit a mother in the leg.

She screamed.

Three masked men rushed in. Held her down. Cut her arms with a knife.

"STOP!" I shouted.

But I realized— With every scream she let out, they hurt her more. And with every word I spoke, he punished them.

Silence became my only weapon. And even that felt useless.

Chapter XLVII

"The hard stuff leaves scars, but the scar is how life remembers how to keep going"-Shani Halimi

I was brought into a room with more men. A stool waited for me. Dark gray table in front. He sat across from me.

His men surrounded us, guns aimed at my head. Nothing new.

"What is your name?" I demanded.

One of them slammed the butt of his gun onto both my hands, pinning them to the table. Pain shot through my bones. If I screamed, I'd die. If I stayed silent... who knew what they'd do.

"Why are you after me?" I asked again.

Another blow. Same gun. Same hands.

My face flushed red from the pain. The room stayed silent. One of the men stepped forward. Ripped the badge from my uniform. Tore it to shreds. Another replaced it. A new badge. A different flag.

Valkros.

I stared at it. Then tore it off myself.

The butt of the gun struck my hands again. Five times. Sharp. Precise. Cruel.

One of them loaded his weapon, aiming.

"Don't," he said. His voice cut through the room. He raised a hand to stop the masked figure.

"Why keep me here if you're not going to kill me?" My voice cracked.

"You don't remember me?" he asked.

"No. Am I supposed to?" My voice echoed in the dark.

He stood. Slowly. Deliberately.

And removed his mask.

Just like my dream.

First, his mouth—lined with a beard creeping toward his lips. Then his nose—straight, tanned, familiar. Finally, the whole mask came off.

I stared.

My breath caught.

"Father?"

Acknowledgements

I began writing this book at the start of my seventh-grade year, driven by a world that holds both war and family—grief and love, chaos and connection. I spent countless hours writing chapter after chapter, pouring my heart into every word. Life isn't picture perfect, and I never expected it to be. But through this story, I've tried to capture both sadness and joy, to reflect the true emotions of bravery, loss, and hope.

Writing this book has been the experience of a lifetime. I sat down, day after day, writing for hours straight. I balanced school, life, and this dream—and somehow, I finished. I don't mind if people don't read my book. Just knowing I published one is enough to make me feel jubilant. That alone is a victory.

To my mom and dad—thank you. You've supported me through this entire voyage, and your belief in me never wavered. To my brothers—you've been my number one fans from the very beginning. I love you endlessly.

To my friends—you didn't think twice before buying my book. Not because I'm your friend, but because you truly believed in me. That means more than you know.

To my extended family, even those living far away—may all your wishes come true. Thank you for helping me discover who I really am, and for making me smile during difficult times. Your love has always reached me, no matter the distance.

To Safta and Papi—I love you. Safta, I never met you, but through the stories I've been told, I see so much of myself in you. Papi, you're in a better place now. May you rest in peace. Your spirit will always be with me. I wish you both were here to see this book, but I've learned that holding on too tightly to what's gone only deepens the ache. Once someone has passed, I carry their memory—not the pain.

To my eighth grade teacher, Mrs. Cowie, thank you for spending months editing my book. You are incredible and I will never forget the things you have done for me to succeed.

To the friends I grew up with—you've been like family from the start. We're all growing up fast, but our memories will always stay the same. Thank you for being part of my story.

I know this book has mistakes, and I know this book isn't perfect. But that was done on purpose. This project is a reflection of my improvement for the years. And I am proud of that.

If you're reading this now, I ask you one thing:

Have a mind with no limits.

As odd as it sounds, I never enjoyed writing growing up. I was always in my own world. I would get scolded for daydreaming, and nighttime would be a blessing because not only am I dreaming, but I am in a new reality.

Dreams can go far into your life. Personally, I find daydreaming to be the key to my success. Without it, I would have never found the story of Alice. I write to escape reality. I write my future, I write my joy and sadness.

I write gold and you can too.

Thank you for the people who have supported me. Thank you for the people who despised me. As crazy as it sounds, the people who have hated me were the people who have pushed me to be the best person I can be today.

With a broken heart, and the loss of a loved one, I walked into middle school with nothing but myself to rely on. Often times, I would cry myself to sleep hoping and wishing life would become easier; that I wouldn't be insecure. For everyone to love me. For me to get away from embarrassment. But G-d never gave me that, and I now know why.

I learned the value of having a few people you can trust rather than thousands.

Life is better when you are yourself. I knew that if my social life changed and I was known widely at my school, I would have to be someone that I wasn't for years. Terrible right?

I'm still a student, but I am much different now. I learned from the past to create my future.

I plan to write many more books throughout my school years, not to prove everyone wrong, but to prove to myself what I'm capable of.

The Playlist That Describes This Book:

1. Solas-Jamie Duffy
2. Viva La Vida-Coldplay
3. Luminary-Joel Sunny
4. Experience-Ludovico Einaudi
5. Je te laisserai des mots-Patrick Watson
6. Lights are on-Tom Rosenthal
7. Take on me-a-ha
8. Another Love-Tom Odell
9. Where'd All the Time Go?-Dr.Dog
10. Ordinary-Alex Warren
11. Sounds Like a Melody 2019 remaster-Alphaville
12. Slipping Through My Fingers-ABBA
13. Forever Young-Alphaville
14. Blue-yung kai
15. End of Beginning-Djo
16. Die With A Smile-Lady Gaga, bruno Mars
17. Hey Soul Sister-Train
18. Sweet Child O'Mine-Guns N'Roses
19. Ticking-TIN
20. Jacob and the Stone-Emile Mosseri
21. Cornfield Chas-Hans Zimmer
22. Idea 10-Gibran Alcocer
23. Riptide-Vance Joy

Thank You